Men's Feet Pie

Carletha Kosky

Copyright © 2017 Carletha Kosky

All rights reserved.

ISBN:13-978-1547200139
ISBN10-1547200138

ACKNOWLEDGMENTS

Thank you to my Mother for believing in me and urging me to tell my stories. Especially this one.

My family, who never wavered in their support of me.

Much gratitude to the people who read this book and gave valuable thoughts and advice. Carlotta Kosky, Barbara Harris Portman Lord, Joyce Felty, and Carol Faye Collins.

And to Jason McKeel, whose art work for the cover of this book was more than just a painting. It captured the true essence of the Pink Pontiac.

Dedication

For Willie and Evelyn Roberts

GOING HOME
1985

      Staring out this window and watching it snow isn't getting me any closer to home. I should be packing right now but I have so many things on my mind that I can't think right. My mind is all jumbled up with so many questions that I can't find the answers to. If only I could go to the River.

      If I was at the River I'm sure that I could get everything figured out. After all, I'm 18 years old and a grown up now, so I should be able to work out all my problems.

      Colorado has pretty mountains, but it doesn't have the River. The town that I grew up in is in Missouri and sits on the banks of the Mississippi. I imagine that Laura Ingalls Wilder probably felt the same way about the Banks of Plum Creek. It was a good place where good things happened, and the bad things never seemed really that bad.

There is something about that big water that makes me feel safe, and a little wild. The water changes every day. Even on the days when the surface is calm, I swear I can still feel the current pulling at me. It is so humid in the summers that you almost can't breathe. In the winter, when ice is floating and the wind is howling, you can look at the water and see the big swirling currents. Everybody I know goes to look at the River at least once a day. And right now, that is where I need to be.

I have some things to say to my family that they are not going to like. I am leaving this town with it's pretty mountains and cool people and going back to the place where I belong. I will be back with Grandma and the River and the rest of the family. As bad as I hate being away, I am dreading the day I get home because for the first time in my life, Grandma is going to be disappointed in me.

Grandma always wanted me to go to college and SEE the WORLD. She said that I would end up back home again, but first I had to get outta the small town before I would ever appreciate it. If I didn't, I would probably be bitter when I was older because I would always feel like I was missing something. She saw the world when she was younger and told me many times that once she got back home, she finally knew who she really was.

I don't really know what that means. I am the first person in my family to go to college and that is really a big deal to everyone, especially Grandma. Nobody is happy that the college is in Denver, which is practically the other side of the world, but that is where the scholarship was, so that is where I went.

I am eighteen years old and the next best thing that I had going for me was working at the Freeze Queen and Grandma was not going to have that. She worked in the sewing factory her whole life, at least until they closed down and sent all of those jobs to China. She said that there was no way I was going to spend my life in a factory or a kitchen cooking for someone else, unless it was for my family.

The day I left home, I went over to say goodbye. She had packed a small cooler and told me not to open it until I got down the road a little way. She slipped me a hundred dollar bill and told me to find a secret place for it and not to tell anyone I had it.

She said that every woman needed her own stash and that I should always remember that. I couldn't believe that she called me a woman. She had always called me her baby until that day. So, I put on a brave face and acted like I was so excited to finally get out and see the world and get a real education. Then she hugged me and said "be careful baby," That's when I started to cry.

Grandpa was out in the yard checking the oil in my car, even though my dad and all of my uncles had already checked it. He was kicking the tires and saw me cry then Grandma started to cry and he said, now "dammit, don't start that. He turned around and ran in to the house. Before he made it inside, I heard him sniffle and saw him wipe his eyes.

It is not just the quitting. Everybody will probably be surprised that I am leaving college, because I have always loved going to school. It all started when I was little and going to the first grade at Immaculate Conception.

I couldn't wait. I knew that school meant that you got to read a lot of books and learn new things and be around interesting people. At least that is what Grandma told me. She used to talk about it all the time when I was over at her house and we were reading.

Of course, she said, you will make lots of new friends and some of the kids on your street will go to the same school as you. I was glad for the friends part of it, but mostly glad that I got to get some new books and read about all the people from a long time ago, like the ones who went West in covered wagons and discovered gold.

I was so excited for first grade. I imagined that my teacher would be just like Miss Beadle in the Little House on the Prairie. Of course I knew that she wouldn't dress the way she did, everybody dresses differently these days, but I figured that she would be pretty and smart and smell like Lemon Verbena, even though I did not know what that smelled like. I figured that I would learn about that smell when I got to school.

The first day I walked in, and I met Sister Bridget, I knew that she was not at all like Miss Beadle. She was wearing a long black robe and had her hair all covered so that you could only see her face. They called it a habit. She met us all in the hallway and then took us to the classroom and pulled out her long wooden yardstick. Some of the kids were crying because they did not want to be in school, and she told them to be silent. When they did not go silent, she smacked her yardstick one time down on the desk. What an awful sound.

Joey Dell started crying harder and she walked right up to his desk and smacked the yardstick up and down on his desk really hard and fast and said that she would hate to accidentally hit him, but she would not stop until he stopped acting like a baby with all his crybaby tears. He was so scared that he stopped crying and peed all over his seat instead. Sister Bridget said "now look at what you just did!" Joey was so ashamed and we all felt ashamed for him. That was when I knew that Sister Bridget was not at all like Miss Beadle, but more like that nasty Mrs. Olsen.

I loved going to school, I just did not like Sister Bridget. I had already learned how to read before I started. My favorite books when I was younger were always about dinosaurs and far away places. Grandma helped me learn my ABC's, and always got me little books. She helped me read about the Little House on the Banks of Plum Creek. I listened to her, and then, before I knew it, I could read the words myself.

I had books in my head all the time. Sometimes, I would be thinking about the Little House and knew that one of these days I was going to be just like Laura Ingalls Wilder. I was going to travel in a wagon with horses, and have a house just like the one they had on the television. I would probably help build it with my own two hands and have a barn full of animals. Even if the Immaculate Conception did not look like the school house, I imagined that it was kind of the same. We used pencils and paper instead of slates, and our books were bigger.

My favorite thing in the world is books. I love the way they smell, the way the pages ripple when you are trying to find your spot, and especially the way they make me feel. When I was little and read a book, I went to places that my imaginations couldn't think up on their own. In my books, I met my secret people, and lived in faraway lands. I ate unusual food. I lived on the Banks of Plum Creek and I traveled across the prairie in a blizzard. I felt the cold and my heart actually pounded when wolves were at the door.

When I was young, books were my best friends, and my best friend of all was the Little House on the Prairie Books. Even though I am eighteen years old now and all grown up, I still feel the same way.

THE RIVER

The first place I am going to go when I pull in to town is the Grotto. It sits right on the River. I need to go there before I go to Grandma's house. I know that everybody will be there waiting for me so I will need to get myself together before I walk in the door.

The Grotto is a stone stacked cave sitting on a small bluff on the levee. It's been there for about a hundred years, and I have heard that one of my great uncles helped to build it. That makes it extra special for me. It's cool to think that my ancestors helped to make the most magical place in town…like I am connected to it in a way that nobody else is.

The doorway is framed in old wood that was probably driftwood at one time. The rocks came from the banks of the River, and the floor is dirt and worn smooth. Only about five people can stand in there comfortably. There is not a back wall or a roof either. When you go in, you have to stoop over a little and then you stand up and the first thing you see is the River swirling. There are vines and ivy and some sort of sweet smelling bush right outside of it. So when you walk in, you feel good, it smells good, and it is mystical feeling.

I always thought that this was the sort of cave that you would come to if you wanted to have a really good talk with God. And to think, this magical place sits on the edge of a town that nobody else has ever heard of, except for the Earthquake. A lot of people have heard about the town of New Madrid because of the big earthquake. In fact, we are all still waiting on another "big one."

They know about the River because it was so powerful that it created a big lake in Tennessee when it ran backwards during the big earthquakes of 1811 and 1812. But they don't know about the River now. Even though the River is not running backwards, it is still the most powerful thing I have ever seen.

I never realized that other kids didn't have a place to go to like the River. I guess that I always took it for granted because I always had it. It was not until I moved away that I realized that I had a little sacred place.

When I was in one of my anthropology classes one day, we were studying Native Americans, and talking about how they had sacred and magical spaces. I never thought about it until the professor asked us if we had a place like that in our own lives. An image of the River and the Grotto came to me all of a sudden and I got so homesick in the middle of class that I had to leave.

Men's Feet Pie

He had told us about pilgrimages and the journey's people make to get to their sacred space and all I could think about was that the whole time I was growing up, we had a little pilgrimage everyday to go to our magical place. We didn't call it a pilgrimage though, we called it circling town.

Circling town was just circling town. You stayed on the main loop through town and made a u-turn at the bottom of the Levee on Main Street to repeat the process until you ran out of gas, or it was time for you to be home. The other end of the loop was the Chat N Chew, a place to get burgers and pizza. So, basically you just made this big circle. While you were circling town, if you wanted to, you could go look at the River. Instead of making the u-turn at the bottom of the Levee, you just continued straight on up and when you got to the top, there it was.

The Big Muddy,….. Mighty Mississippi,…The River. Then you could drive along the top of the levee, where you would pass the Grotto and then keep on going and come down the Levee on the other side of town. Friday and Saturday nights were bumper to bumper on Main Street.

Your parents teach you how to circle town, because they grew up in the town and they did it when they were teenagers. When you were a baby and couldn't get to sleep, you were likely put in to the car and taken to see The River until you fell asleep. Whenever there was a fight in the family, somebody always said, "I'm gonna go look at the River." That gave them someplace to go until things calmed down. If somebody had an important piece of news, they said let's go look at The River.

I guess the River is kind of important if I miss it that much.

Now, I am leaving College and Colorado forever and I guess I am making a Big Pilgrimage home to my Sacred Place. When I get there, even before I go to see Grandma , I am going to go straight to the Grotto and have a talk with God. Then I will be able to tell Grandma and the rest of the family that I am quitting school forever because I just can't cut it. And, I should have been at home these last couple of months instead of a thousand miles away. If I had been home, maybe things would be different now.

It is almost Christmas Time, and that is the best time of the year in my family. But this time Christmas won't be the same. Too many things have changed.

Right now, I need to get my car packed and get on the road. The only thing that could have stopped me from going home was a blizzard. But, a blizzard never arrived so I packed up my Cutlass Supreme and took everything in my room. I grabbed my books and took my posters off the wall. Then, when I was pulling the sheets off the bed and getting my pillow all stuffed in the bag it hit me. One of the things I missed about home was the way everything smelled.

The sheets in my dorm room didn't smell like the sheets at home. I miss the smell of laundry. Not just any laundry, but the way that white t-shirts always smell when you fold them just out of the dryer.

And sheets. There was a certain smell that fresh washed sheets always had when you shook them out and put them on the bed. We never bothered to fold the sheets, just took them straight out of the dryer and put them on the bed.

Washing clothes at the laundromat doesn't give the clothes the same smell as washing them at home. Anyway, I don't know why I am thinking about stuff like this. I guess because my quilt that I had on the bed did not smell like the quilts at Grandma's house. And I want that again.

Some of the other girls in the dorm talked about being homesick, and missing people. I missed the people in my family and my friends, of course, but I really got that feeling of homesickness whenever I remembered things that had to do with a song, or a smell, or certain words.

I got in the car and realized that I am gritting my teeth just like my dad always does when he is stressed out. Grandma used to say that one of these days he was gonna show up for supper with no teeth left to chew his food with. So, thinking about those pearls of wisdom, I guess I better get some gum or something, because the drive is long and I am sure that I am gonna grit my teeth for the next 18 hours.

I wonder if this is how Laura Ingalls felt?

Probably not. She had her family with her the whole time. As much as Grandma always wanted me to be close to her, she was the one who insisted that I leave and not come back until I finished college. So, I left on a scholarship and got into the car to drive 1000 miles away to get an education and SEE THE WORLD. I saw everything I wanted to in a few months. I made the decision that when I went home for Christmas, I was not going back to Colorado.

Well, it is not quite Christmas, but I am pulling up and getting out of here early. I might go somewhere else, but Colorado is just too far and the thought of staying here for four years makes me feel sick. I felt better after I decided, but then I knew what would happen when I went home.

My dad would be happy and tell me that I should have never left. Mom would tell me that I had to find my own "path." She was always saying that. I could just imagine her with her big bell bottomed pants on and her big scarf talking about it.

She always talks about "paths" and that everybody has to be true to themselves and not do what society thinks you should do. My dad never thought that we should do what society tells you either, but we "had better damn well do whatever he tells us to do."

But my Grandma was going to be very disappointed.

If my best friend Maria was with me, we would pop in the cassette of John Cougar and sing the whole way home. Our favorite song was Jack and Diane ...doing the best they can. But, she isn't with me and I really don't feel much like singing anyway. So, starting my car, I only have one thing on my mind. I'm going home.

FAMILY

     Grandma's yard smells like honeysuckle. She and Grandpa live off a gravel road, so the plants on that side of the house are always dusty, but the dust can't cover up that honeysuckle smell. Grandpa was a carpenter his whole life. Well, not his whole life. He was also a medic during World War 2, but since I did not know him then, I guess he has been a carpenter for my whole life. He liked to build houses, sheds, barns, and other buildings, but mostly he liked to build shelves for Grandma.
     He had this old car that was the color of Pepto Bismal. It was a 1957 Pink Pontiac and he drove it everywhere. He took the backseats out and that is where he kept his tools in their wooden boxes that he made. The car was always full of cut pieces of wood and had a really old radio in it without a cassette player. It was so old that it didn't even have an 8 track.
     The front seat was all white leather. I loved

the way that car smelled on the inside....like sawdust and Old Spice, which was also the way Grandpa smelled. I also liked it whenever he started that car up because on the outside, it smelled like exhaust. Maria thought I was nuts because I like to smell that exhaust whenever the car started up.

Grandpa hauled a lot of wood in that car to his house to make the shelves for Grandma. I'm not talking about something to put pretties on either. Grandma had this bedroom in the middle of her house that she used to store food in. She called it Puttin' By, which meant that she never wanted to run out of food. Shelves lined every wall in this bedroom and they were all full of canned food in glass jars that my Grandma or my aunts grew.

She had a huge garden in her back yard and she had some fruit trees too. Right outside the kitchen was this Granny Smith Apple tree that had sour apples that we couldn't get enough of. We used those to make fried pies. She had a plum tree, a peach tree and three fig bushes. Aunt Darcy grew tons of turnips and potatoes and onions, but if anyone wanted any they had to go dig them up themselves and leave a couple of jars of whatever they grew. So, in addition to the shelves, Grandpa built these wooden bins that held turnips and potatoes. For the onions, Grandma used panty hose hung from nails that were in the closet in the room. She would drop in an onion, then a quick twist and a rubber band and then she would drop in another onion and continue doing that until it looked like giant beaded necklaces were hanging from the ceiling.

    The day I left, there wasn't anyone else at their house. It was strange, because they always had somebody over, no matter what time of the day or night. They had five kids and a whole bunch of grandkids and everybody went to grandma and grandpa's house. I guess I was special because I was the first grandchild. They had one girl and 4 boys. My mom was the only girl.

    Mom met my dad when she was in high school. Dad was a total greaser. He rode a Harley and had cigarettes rolled up in his white t-shirt, just like The Fonze. He also had a tattoo on his arm, a big blue one that just said one word. Mom.

    He had quit high school when he was in the tenth grade. Anyway, Grandma hated my dad because he drove too fast and didn't have a prospect in this world. And also because he came from the wrong town. Even though the town was only 4 miles away, to Grandma it was another world and she did not think that he was good enough for her baby. My dad also likes to cuss, which Grandma doesn't like.

    She tried to talk my mom into going out with a boy from our own town, or even moving so that she could get an education. Mom would have none of that. Grandma even offered to send her to California so that she could go to acting school and become a famous actress if she would just leave Wild Joey Brzinsky.

    My mom did the only thing she could think of to marry to man of her dreams. She snuck out of the house and they ran off to St. Louis.

She was still in high school at the time and Grandma somehow found her and told her that if she would just come home and finish school that she would give them a wedding. Grandma thought that mom would change her mind.

She tried to help with changing her mind by always introducing her to good boys with "prospects." But, nobody else would do for my mom. She loved her wild man. Even though he had no prospects, he did have a Harley and was the coolest guy in town.

So, they got married in a church, with the parents on both sides gritting their teeth. Mom's parents thought that he was no good and dad's mom thought that he was getting into a family of snobs.

Nine months later, I was born and it changed everything. Of course, Grandma was mad at Dad for getting her baby pregnant, and all during the pregnancy, Grandma worried and fussed. She couldn't believe that Mom was going to have "his child." I'm sure that she imagined a baby boy coming out with a leather jacket and a cigarette hanging out of his mouth. Instead, I showed up.

All of a sudden, my dad did something right. I had his eyes. But then, a whole new set of problems came up. Grandma thought that my mom was much too young to be a mother and couldn't possibly take care of me the right way. She got nervous when mom gave me a bath, told her that she was holding the bottle wrong when she fed me and never thought that she dressed me pretty enough. She also kept telling Mom that my Dad better get a good job, or I was gonna grow up with bad teeth and getting made fun of. Grandma thought that she should just keep me at her house all the time.

Mom finally had enough one day after a vicious fight over my mom not burping me right. Mom and Dad ran away to St. Louis again, but this time I was in the car with them. Mom snuggled me down in the laundry basket in the back seat with all of their clothes and took off. It broke my Grandma's heart. She decided that she would be nicer to my Dad and let Mom raise me the way she wanted to if they would just come home.

So, Mom and Dad went home, partially because Mom missed her brothers and the rest of the family. The uncles on my mom's side of the family are all very different from each other. The only thing they had in common was that they all thought that Grandma had a favorite, and that it wasn't them.

It was kind of funny hearing all of them talk about who was the favorite. Grandpa would just shake his head and laugh in his quiet way whenever he heard one of them say that. I asked him one day if he thought Grandma had a favorite kid. He said "sure she does."

"It is whichever kid is the sickest, the furthest away, or in the most trouble at the time. It has been each one of the kids at some time or another." "See," he said, "your Grandma is gonna give the most attention to the one who needs her most. And, I'm sure that she is gonna be like this even when they are all grown up."

I have a huge family. I am the oldest and I

have one sister and one brother. But that is not the whole family. Grandma has eight sisters and two brothers and Grandpa has seven sisters and three brothers. They all had big families too. Cousins everywhere.

My dad has five brothers and sisters, so I was always surrounded by family and Sundays were the day that everybody went over to Grandma's house to eat.

The oldest is Uncle Charlie. He's a calm one. He takes after Grandpa in the way they look and walk. He joined the military when he just got out of high school. We don't get to see him very often, and whenever he comes around he spends most of his time hanging out with Grandpa.

They don't really do anything, they just sit quiet with each other without really talking much. That seems to be ok with both of them and nobody really interferes with them while they are just sitting and doing nothing. Even though they don't say anything, it always seems like they are having some kind of conversation.

I think it is because Grandpa was in the Army during World War 2 and Uncle Charlie was in a place called Saigon. That is something they have in common with each other, both of them being in the Army. Sometimes they do actually talk with words, but the kids can't hear because we are too young and would not understand, at least that is what Grandma says.

It is really odd the way Grandma acts, 'cause she is involved in almost all the conversations her kids have, but she leaves uncle

Charlie's conversations to just Grandpa. Mom says that Uncle Charlie was always quiet, but when he got back, he just wasn't the same.

I remember once, there was a bunch of us kids over at Grandma and Grandpa's place and we actually heard Uncle Charlie say more than just a few words.

He had only been back from the Army for a couple of months and was still getting used to being back home. We were in the living room and heard him yelling. We ran in to the kitchen and heard him say "Oh, momma please don't. You don't understand".

Grandma told him not to bother looking in his room for any more. She had searched all over in his room and in the bathroom and found every one of the bottles he had stashed. Grandma was standing at the sink pouring a bottle of booze right down the drain. She was shaking and said "I won't have it in my house."

Uncle Charlie just sat at the kitchen table and cried like a baby. Right then, Grandpa came in and swooped up Uncle Charlie and walked him out to his car. He said "we are going to look at the River." They stayed gone for hours.

I told my mom what happened later and she said that Uncle Charlie came back from the war a broken man. The army got a sweet good boy and turned him in to an empty shell then sent him home. She was afraid that no amount of love or good food was ever going to fix him. She said that the bottle became his best friend and the only person who could help him was probably Grandpa.

She said a lot of good boys came back from Vietnam like that. At least Charlie wasn't violent. We had that to be thankful for. Grandma had told her that when Grandpa came back from fighting in the Pacific he was hell to be around for a really long time. He drank a lot too, but eventually he calmed down.   We can only hope that the old Uncle Charlie comes back.

Uncle Lee is the next uncle. My mom is older than him. He is really serious and quiet, just like Grandpa. He got a job bagging groceries at the IGA when he was in High School, and worked his way up to assistant manager. He has a wife and two kids. Even though nobody talks about it, we all know that he got a girl "in trouble" when they were in high school so they had to get married. After she had the baby, it wasn't too long that they got "in trouble" again, but this time it was no big deal because they were married. The babies were both boys, and Grandma said that they would be best friends 'cause they were so close in age. Anyway, Uncle Lee is quiet, works hard, and we only see him on Sundays at supper because he works all the time. He has straight hair.

Hair is an important thing in our family. We have the straight hairs, and the curly hairs. Usually the straight headed ones are polite and never cause trouble. The curly hairs are a different story. In our family, everybody knows that if a kid has curly hair, you should expect some mischief from them when they are young, and probably trouble with the law when they get older. It always happens. The calm straight-headed ones help to get them out of trouble.

Grandma gets mad whenever the subject of curly hairs and straight hairs comes up. The stories about the curly hairs and the straight hairs go way back generations on my Grandma's side of the family. One day, one of my cousins was acting up and his dad didn't get on to him.

Grandma asked why he wasn't getting a spanking and my Uncle Lee said "he can't help it, he has curly hair." She said "that is just stupid, you gotta discipline that kid and not let him get away with that crap just 'cause he has curly hair." She said "the curly hairs aren't all vices and the straight hairs aren't all virtues." I think that means that everybody has both good and bad in them.

Now, on the subject of hair, we also have a streak of red hair that runs on both sides of the family, but you never know when it is gonna pop up. The red haired ones are always admired cause the red is a beautiful deep and rich color. If somebody had red hair and curls, you never knew what to expect, but life would be exciting whenever they were around.

I never fit in to any category. My hair wasn't straight, but it wasn't exactly curly either. It was not blond or red, but kind of golden reddish color that they called strawberry blond. I had big waves in my hair so it always looked kind of messy. I always kept it cut in Angel Wings, just like Farrah Fawcett on Charlies Angels. Aunt Darcy said that meant that I wanted to be good, but would probably find trouble more often than not. Grandma said that was a ridiculous notion.

Back to the Uncles. His real name is

William, but we call him Uncle Billy. He is funny and kind of wild. He has a different girlfriend every week, and women lined up for a chance to go out with him. He is what Grandma calls a heartbreaker. His hair is brown, but so curly that you cannot get a comb through it. And the women can't get enough of him. Grandma says he will probably never settle down. It will take a really special woman to hold on to him, but he will always have a wandering eye.

Then there is Uncle Jake, who is the baby of the family. He is another Curly hair and boy does he find trouble. He can be just about anywhere and be totally innocent, but somehow will have an encounter with the law, or a jealous husband, or a mad woman. It never fails. If I was him, I would probably just stay home, and I told him that one day. He said that wouldn't help, cause trouble will come knocking on his door.

All this thinking about my family is making me more anxious to get home. I better get started on the road home, and while I drive, I will have plenty of time to think about everybody.

The car is loaded. I drove to the gas station to fill up, got some pork rinds and beef jerky for the road and the last thing to do was to use the pay phone to call my dad and let him know that I am getting on the road. I always had to call collect because it would take to many quarters to make my calls. He answered the phone on the first ring. I could tell by his voice that he was nervous about me driving home all that way by myself.

When I left for college, they loaded everybody in the station wagon and followed me out to Colorado. He reminded me to check the oil and have someone at the gas station make sure that the tires were aired up. We didn't say much more than that, but he told me that I need to call them the next time that I stopped for gas.

He went down the list of things that he tells me every time that I talk to him. Don't pick up hitch hikers, pull over if I get sleepy, and watch the speed. "Don't you dare go over 55 miles an hour." Then with his final advice to lock the door as soon as I get in to the car, I tell him I gotta go.

All filled up and everything checked, it was time to hit the road. As soon as I pulled on to the interstate I start thinking about my own family.

I am the oldest. A fact that I was never able to forget because every time I did something wrong, I was told "you are the oldest! You have to set the example for your sister." Then, when Willie was born, it became "you are the oldest! You have to set the example for your sister and brother too!"

Everybody calls me Sis. I have a younger

sister named Bobbie Sue and a little brother we call Willie, but Grandma always called him Billy Jo. He was named after my uncle, but William was too grown up of a name to call him when he was little.

I remember when he was born. It was 1974, my Mom and Bobbie Sue and I were in the Brown Station Wagon going over to Grandma's house. Our favorite song came on the radio and mom turned it up.

BJ Thomas was singing Hooked on a Feeling and we were all singing with him when mom slammed on the brakes. My sister was 4 years old and in the back of the station wagon singing at the top of her lungs. She bounced off the back glass and then back into the back seat and looked up to start crying. Mom just said "it's time."

We sat there for a few minutes then she said "we had to get to Grandma's real quick so that we can call dad." With that song playing and all of us singing, mom got us to Grandma's house as fast as we could. I don't remember him actually being born, but I remember all of us singing that song that day. Every time that song comes on the radio, I think of him.

It is funny how songs and certain foods make you remember something from long ago. Since I am 18 years old and a grownup now, you would think that I forgot all that stuff. But one whiff of a food or a certain song makes me feel like I am back at that place where I first heard it or smelled the food.

Food is a big thing in my family. It is the reason we all get together on the weekends. Food is big during the week too, but that is when everybody has their own home dinners. And the food is just your normal dinner. I never realized until I started eating over at friend's houses that I came from a family of particular eaters. Food was the center and source of nearly every family function. At the dinner table was where we learned about manners. Good manners would get you nearly anything and out of trouble. Bad manners would get you banned.

We learned not to smack our food or to chew too loud. At the dinner table was where we had our worst family fights and shared our happiest moments. Secrets were exposed and pacts were made. Sometimes, all of those things happened during one meal.

For one thing, everybody in the family, down to the littlest kid, has an opinion on their food and how the favorite should be cooked. It is not that we were picky eaters, but we just had our own ways of doing things. Some really bad arguments actually started over food and one that has gone on in the family for years is the argument about Hellmans vs. Miracle Whip.

There have been times when this argument has turned violent. Every Saturday, somebody had a big meal at their house. It switched up depending on who was working or who wanted to have it. This is when even the out of town cousins came in to visit.

One year, on the Fourth of July, Aunt Millie had a big to-do at her house. The cousins and aunts and uncles came from all over the place even as far away as Indiana. And everyone brought something, or brought their ingredients over to Aunt Millie's house so that they could cook there.

The men had about 4 bbq grills going because there was so much meat to cook. And the women were all in the house getting the other stuff ready. Somebody had snatched a deviled egg off of one of the plates and the word spread like wildfire…Miracle Whip.

Thankfully, there were other plates and when Little Zack snagged one, he ran out to tell everyone that the white plate with flowers on it was Hellmans. We all cheered. So, everyone knew what plate to take their deviled eggs from.

But, that day, something else happened. We all knew that Aunt Millie had problems with corns on her feet. She was always talking about how much they hurt and how she tried to pull them off. She grossed everyone out because she would sit in her chair and pick at them.

Aunt Millie was in the kitchen mixing up coleslaw but she wasn't using a spoon. She was using her bare hands. My Mom was disgusted and said "I hope that you haven't been picking at your corns, because that is just plain nasty. Use a spoon!"

Aunt Millie looked at her hands and made a big show of checking under her fingernails dripping with mayonnaise and said. "You know, I did pick at some corns last night and as hard as I tried, I could not get them from underneath my fingernails. Looks like Hellmans does the trick. I don't see any sign of them now."

Well, Aunt Bert and Aunt Millie always

had an uneasy relationship. They were polite to each other, but you could tell that was as far as they were willing to go. Aunt Bert brought over the ingredients for the coleslaw because she is another one in the family that insisted on Hellman's for everything.

She knew that if she did not bring Hellman's, somebody would use Miracle Whip and then there would be hell to pay. She was going to make the coleslaw but Aunt Millie beat her to it so she had to watch Aunt Millie make it instead of doing it herself. She got so mad that she picked up a spoon and threw it at Aunt Millie and hit her right in the back and said "you better be kidding!"

Aunt Millie just turned to look at her and said "Don't worry, it can only improve the taste. If I had used Miracle Whip, there wouldn't be any need for extra corns in the coleslaw." Before we knew what was happening, they were at each other. First, there was just pushing and pulling, somehow, it ended up outside where all the men and the kids were. We all thought it was just a joke, but Aunt Bert had a temper like my dad and took it a little too far. She took Aunt Millie straight to the ground. They had a wrestling match right outside on the Fourth of July that seemed to last forever.

We didn't just argue over the mayo though. There were other foods that were insisted on, depending on who's house you were at.

One time, My dad asked Uncle Lee if he would mind bringing over some sandwich food for us kids on Saturday morning because he got called in to work that day and didn't have time to go to the store. He gave him some money and told him to get a loaf of bread and some salami and bologna and some mayonnaise. Just to make sure that he understood, my dad reminded him about the mayo. Don't you dare bring any Miracle Whip in to this house. Get real mayonnaise… Hellman's!

So, Uncle Lee did as he was asked and brought in all the food in brown IGA sacks. I started to unload all the groceries and fold up the paper sacks. I pulled the bread out of the last sack when my dad walked in the door from work early. When I saw the loaf, I knew there would be trouble, because I knew about my dad's opinion on bread.

He saw the loaf wrapper with the bunny on it and just stared at it and then glared at my Uncle Lee, who was innocent of course, because he did not live in our house and didn't know the rules about what bread we used.

All of a sudden, Dad threw his hands up in the air and screamed "Bunny Bread….goddammed Bunny Bread!" "I can believe you brought that in to this house. That shit tastes like dough and I can never get it out of my teeth. Go back to the store and get some Wonder Bread." With that being said, dad picked up the Bunny Bread and smashed it down in to the trash can.

The kind of bread you use depends on how you take your bologna. In our family, there is a side of the family who likes it cold on a sandwich with mayo and the other half who will not touch bologna unless it is fried first, and always served with Hellman's on both sides of the bread. I like my bologna fried. It tastes better and gets the bread a little greasy. The grease mixes perfectly with Hellman's and makes a perfect sandwich. I understand my dad getting mad about the bread , because Bunny Bread will not hold up with fried bologna. It has to be Wonder, or you might as well just have cold bologna and crackers.

There were a few mustard people in the family, but they were all related by marriage and stayed out of the arguments. Nobody really took the mustard people seriously anyway. They would usually just eat whatever was on the table and have no opinion about it either way.
I never really understood people that did not care about what food they ate. Some of my friends just ate whatever and really never talked about their favorite thing.

In our family, you always got your favorite on your birthday and everybody knew what was going to be cooking. My favorite meal is ham-n-beans. Growing up, if someone said that we were having beans for supper, what they really meant was that we were having ham and beans, fried potatoes, and cornbread with fresh butter. To go along with it was always a big plate with onion chunks and some collard greens. The thought of having ham and beans without those other items was unheard of. It's funny how some people eat. I have been to other people's homes, where they had ham and beans for supper, and all they did was open up a couple of cans and chop up a canned ham and put it in.

Ham and beans always started the night before in our house. First, the dried beans were put in a big pot and placed on the back of the stove to soak all night. Then, the big ham bone that was leftover from some meal was taken out of the freezer to thaw for the next day. The next morning, the bacon would be frying in the cast iron skillet because no self-respecting cook would dare make ham and beans without bacon grease. Or fry potatoes in anything but bacon grease, or grease the bottom of the cornbread pan with anything other than bacon grease. The beans would cook all day so that the broth was nice and thick and just perfect for dunking a piece of potato or a chunk of cornbread slathered with butter. I don't ever remember a time when we went to Grandma's house to eat that there wasn't a big bouquet of green onions in a mason jar of water sitting on the table, sliced white bread and soft butter to spread all over it.

There is one rule about food that every single person in the family agreed on and that is butter. No margarine in plastic tubs for us. It had to be butter or we would just do without. Grandpa always enjoyed his butter so much. He used to tell us that when he was growing up that all they had was lard to put on their biscuits, and that they were thankful to have that much. Once he had a family of his own, he was going to make sure that there was bread and butter on the table every meal.

While I am doing all of this thinking and remembering about the family, an image of Aunt Darcy came to me and I busted out laughing in my car all by myself. I loved all of my family, but after Mom and Dad and Grandpa and Grandma, I loved

Aunt Darcy the best. She is my Grandma's sister so that makes her a great-aunt. But we all just called her Aunt Darcy.

Aunt Darcy is funny, but only because she doesn't know how funny she is. She has this wild mass of blonde hair, full of ringlets and curls and kind of fuzzy because she doesn't use conditioner. It falls way down past her shoulders and always looks kind of crazy, like she was in the middle of teasing it and forgot to put it up. Everyone said that she was eccentric, but I didn't care. She had opinions on everything and the way she could tell a story always made me laugh. Aunt Darcy played the guitar and loved to sing Joan Baez songs all the time.

During the summer, we were usually at her house 2 or 3 days a week for a visit. She has this porch that wraps around the whole front of her house. Part of it sagged on one side, but she said that was ok, that was the cat side of the porch and they didn't mind. She had a bunch of old lawn furniture piled high with pillows on the sagging side and even if you couldn't see the cats, with them all laying there purring there was a constant hum from that side. Aunt Darcy always had some kind of stray animal at her house that she was feeding or doctoring up. And it seemed like she had about 100 cats scattered all over the place. She would sit on that porch playing her guitar and singing folk songs while the cats hummed and purred.

We would go and play while her and Grandma sat on the porch and shelled beans, or shucked corn and talked. I don't know how they never ran out of things to talk about.

She had a lot of opinions on the government, but usually Grandma would shut her up when she got on the subject of wars. Aunt Darcy went to a lot of protests and sit-ins over the war in Vietnam. She said that she was usually the oldest one there, but also the one with the most sense. She is one that they called "back-to-land'ers."

She lived on a couple of acres right outside of town and had chickens and gardens everywhere. Well, she called them gardens. My dad called them big weed patches. She kept everybody supplied in turnips in the fall and other stuff throughout the summer. She grew odd things like horseradish. She had bought a piece of horseradish at the grocery store once and decided to plant it to see if anything would come up. Sure enough, she grew horseradish. She would divvy that out amongst the family. Nobody ate it, but we all told her that we did, on some good roast beef. Everybody hated the way it tasted, especially Aunt Darcy. But she continued to grow it, and we pretended to eat it and nobody got mad.

Aunt Darcy would make a big show of grating it by hand with her rusty cheese grater. She would always tear up and get watery eyes and a runny nose when she grated the horseradish, but she insisted on doing it. One day, she had the brilliant idea of putting on swimming goggles and a clothespin on her nose while she was grating the horseradish.

Grandma told her that she looked ridiculous and started laughing the first time she saw her do this, but Aunt Darcy got so mad and told Grandma that she was going doing it *for Her* and if she did not appreciate the gesture then she would stop supplying horseradish for the family. I could tell that Grandma had a hard time keeping a straight face, because Aunt Darcy was wearing her goggles and clothespin while she was saying all of this so the words came out funny. But she was so serious that we both stopped laughing.

Even though Grandma hated the taste of the stuff, she quickly said "Oh no Darcy…I'm sorry. We love the horseradish." Later, when Grandma was driving us home, I asked her why she didn't take the chance to stop with the horseradish. She said that sometimes you need to do that in families. Keep your mouth shut about something you hated if your sister loved it. She had seen families torn apart by something as simple as horseradish before and was not going to let that happen to us. "Plus, Aunt Darcy would go into a depression for months and I would never hear the end of it." So, we were all going to have to live with horseradish for the rest of our lives or until Aunt Darcy decided to quit growing it.

She planted stuff everywhere, but the only problem was that she forgot what seeds she put where, and then would not weed anything in case she accidentally pulled up a "good plant."In fact, she never weeded anything, so her yard looked like a mess of a jungle most of the summer. Then, in the fall, everything would die off but she would not mow it down because she wanted to let it naturally fertilize the ground for next spring's planting.

Her place was always knee high in something or other and my mom didn't like for any of us to play in her yard, because we might step on a snake or a nesting chicken or something.

One year, a couple of goats showed up and ate everything that she had planted right to the ground. I thought she was going to have a conniption, but instead she decided to take up goats and try her hand at making goat cheese and lotions out of their milk. She never made any lotion and after her first attempt at making cheese she quit. I was there with Grandma the day she made that cheese. She was so proud because it was pretty and white and looked really good.

When it was finished, she had small loaves of cheese that she arranged on her prettiest china. She sliced off a piece for everybody and served it on saltine crackers. She said that she might become a cheese maker and sell it. Then, with a flourish she put the whole cracker in her mouth and so did me and Grandma. I knew immediately that something was very wrong with that cheese.

Before I could spit mine out, Aunt Darcy started gagging and crackers flew out of her mouth. Grandma's eyes were tearing up but she didn't want to offend Aunt Darcy, so she kept chewing. Grandma just stared at me and I remembered what she said about not upsetting Aunt Darcy over the horseradish so I tried to hold my breath.

I tried, really I did.

But before I knew it, that mushy nasty cheese started coming out of my mouth with bits of saltine cracker. Aunt Darcy lost hers at the same time. Not Grandma. She swallowed and I was amazed at how much she must love her sister to swallow that rotten tasting stuff. Thankfully, Aunt Darcy decided to never make goat cheese again. She said that it didn't taste like it was supposed to.

After she got the goats, she went through planting stuff, only to have the goats eat it right down to the ground. She would yell at the goats, and then plant more stuff.

She was another one who insisted on good manners. She always had a saying, "class isn't something you wear, but something you have. And classy people don't fart in earshot of other people!"

Farts offended her like nothing else could. If any one of the kids farted, she would turn red and start shaking her head then stalk out of the offensive room, slamming every door that she could till she got outside. She even got upset when one of her goats farted once. I was there the day that happened.

This old goat farted and just stared at Aunt Darcy. She got all upset and told him not to do it again. He just stood there chewing on his cud and let out another. Aunt Darcy turned around and walked off. She wouldn't look at him for days. The goat didn't care though. Grandma always laughed at Aunt Darcy because she had such a bad and unexpected temper. You never knew what she would find funny, but you also never knew what would set her off.

My favorite story about Aunt Darcy is the time she decided to come and stay with us for a week.

At my house, we had a living room that everybody would pile up in. Next to the living room was the kitchen and then the added on part of the house that was my dad's room.

We called it "his" room because that is where he always went to sit and watch tv. He had a pool table in there and a small card table in the corner where he would play cards with his buddies every Friday night when they got off work. Next to the card table were the bird cages.
My dad loved birds. Not pretty little songbirds, but instead he had big squawking pooping birds that could talk.

They are called African Greys and he had two of them. Those birds could mimic any sound that they ever heard and could say a lot of words too. Usually it was stuff they heard my dad or his buddies say over and over again. Or the sounds they made. The men would grunt and burp and fart all they wanted, because that is what men do when they play cards. Those birds cussed a lot. It always upset my mom, but Dad would swear that they must have learned those words before he got them.

A tree limb fell off a tree during a storm one day and knocked a hole through Aunt Darcy's roof. She showed up with a basket full of 3 day old kittens and the momma cat and announced that she would be staying with us for a few days until her roof was patched up. She stayed in my room, and I was going to sleep on the couch. She wanted to keep the kittens and momma cat in the room if she had to step out for a while. Those kittens were so tiny that they looked like little mice.

I was in the living room watching tv with Willie, Bobbie Sue, and my little cousins Bryn and Zack, and Aunt Darcy decided she wanted to go in the back room and watch a little TV herself. She took momma cat with her and they settle in dad's recliner to watch The Young and Restless. I heard her saying something, in a really loud voice.

I went in to investigate and found her yelling at the birds and telling them to watch their mouths. The birds were singing a pretty little tune but all the words were cuss words, and I mean the bad cuss words. The little cousins followed me in to see what was going on.

We were all standing in the doorway watching this when one of the birds let out a really long farting sound.

We all knew how she felt about that and we did not know what to expect from her. She might be calm or she might just knock over both of the bird cages. Or she might open the door and let the birds loose to go fart elsewhere. She tried to ignore it but then the other bird started laughing and sounded just like my dad laughing. The more one laughed, the more the other one made fart sounds until Aunt Darcy could take no more.

She got redder and redder and snatched up the cat and screamed all the way to my bedroom about the damned farts in this house and Joe Brzinsky was going to get it for teaching his birds to fart and then laugh about it. She slammed every door she could see on the way down the hallway. The bathroom door didn't slam loud enough so she opened it up and slammed it again for good measure. Then she slammed the door to my room and managed to sputter out that she was not to be disturbed. She needed a nap because she was worn out.

We could hear her cussing and talking to herself in there for about an hour until she finally settled down to go to sleep. We all went back to watching TV. Gilligan's Island was on and The Brady Bunch was up next, so the little kids were anxious to get back to it.

Grandpa had stopped over to drop off some tools for my dad so he stayed for some tea until dad got there. My dad came in from work with a sack of candy bars for all of us kids and was talking to Grandpa when all of a sudden Aunt Darcy slams open the door to my bedroom and stalks out.

Now, this is the last thing my dad expected, because he didn't even know she was staying with us. Plus, he was kind of afraid of Aunt Darcy because he never knew what she was going to say or do.

Her hair was crazy wild and sticking out all over the place and she started screaming at my dad. She was waving her hands around and then gave it to him in her highest pitch voice.

"What kind of a man keeps cussing birds around small children and did you try to teach them to fart, or did they just learn it from your card playing friends, and if that is the case you need to get some new friends because no self-respecting man would let his friends fart around his kids!!"

My dad just stood there with his mouth open and Grandpa calmly sipped his tea. Grandpa had seen these fits plenty of times, and never got worked up whenever Aunt Darcy went into one of her conniptions. The momma cat started yowling at her feet and trying to jump up on her. Normally, momma cat stays away from her when she is like this, but she was yowling so loud that Aunt Darcy stopped screaming long enough to say "now you hush."

My cousins and I had mouths full of chocolate and my little cousin Bryn says "oh, Aunt Darcy she wants her babies." Aunt Darcy says "her babies are fine, they are all sleeping in the basket at the foot of the bed."

Grandpa reached over and plucked a little 3 day old kitten out of Aunt Darcy's hair. Then another one fell out and Grandpa caught it before it hit the floor. All of a sudden, her hair was alive with the sounds of kittens mewling for their mother and for the first time in her life, Aunt Darcy was left speechless. All of the kittens had nested in her hair as she slept and some were so hopelessly tangled up that we had to help get them out.

Once the kittens were freed and put back in the basket, Aunt Darcy had run out of steam. She was so upset that the kittens were stuck in her hair that she didn't know what to do. I thought she was going to hyperventilate she was breathing so hard. She picked up the basket, threw momma cat on top and said that she was going home, roof or not. At least she wouldn't have to put up with those damned farting birds anymore.

Before she left, she told all of us kids in her most serious voice that we "should not ever practice manners that we learned from a bird." Then with a glare at my dad, she was out the door.

In the background, we could all hear the birds still laughing and farting in the back room.

Right after she left, Mom came home from the beauty shop and walked in the house. Dad was still upset at being ambushed by Aunt Darcy and started in on mom about letting that crazy woman come over and not warning him about it and that the kids were going to have nightmares about "kittens in the hair" from now on.

There are so many stories about Aunt Darcy. She was always at family gatherings, and stopped by the house all the time to drop off something she grew or made. She never had any kids of her own, but she loved being around all of us, at least that is what she said.

She thought it was her job to teach us about things that she thought were important. Sometimes, though it was confusing because she said that we should respect our elders, but then in the next breath she told us to question authority. Now, how does that even make sense?

THE BRYZINSKYS

My mom has a beauty shop. She never planned on having one, it just happened that way. She always thought that she would be part of the flower power movement and go to music concerts and protests with Aunt Darcy. She thought that she would like to be a poet and write songs. I remember hearing them talking about the war in Vietnam.

That was before she met my dad though. She started doing hair right before I was born. She learned how by watching others do hair. She knew practically everyone in town. She had this big corkboard on the wall in her beauty shop that had tons of pictures of little kids getting their first hair cut. She gave most of my friends their first cuts when they were babies, and also did up all of our hair for things like dances and proms.

My mom is really pretty and smiles a lot. She looks different than most of the other moms because she wears platform shoes and bell bottom pants and caftans. She usually has some sort of scarf tied around her head or her waist and wears a lot of macramé jewelry that she makes herself.

I spent a lot of time at the beauty shop with her, in fact all of us did. There was this one kind of hairdo that she did that fascinated me every time I saw her do it. It's called a beehive. She would start off with a can of hairspray and somehow tease it up until it looked like some monster with hair sticking out all over the place. Then she would do some sort of magic swoop with her hand and the next thing that you knew the hair was standing in a perfect form that looked to be about three feet tall on the woman's head. She did a lot of rollers and sets for the older women in town, and she did perms all day long for the younger people.

I have seen some strange things happen in her beauty shop. I remember this one time a lady came in and was all bristly and mad. She snapped at everyone and got mad at some kids who were spinning in one of the chairs. Well, mom got her in the chair pretty quick to do her rollers and set. My mom was really calm while all of this was going on.

She was upset and mad about something and talking loud and looking at my mom in the mirror. Then she burst into tears and mom stopped long enough to hand her a tissue, but kept right on rolling that hair. Pretty soon, the woman calmed down, and started telling her story.

Mom would just nod her head. Hair in

rollers, she went to sit under the dryer to get the good set. By the time the hair was dry and the woman back in my mom's chair, the conversation would continue right where it left off. Before long, the hair was done up in a perfect set and the woman was laughing as she got up and shook herself out of the cape. I saw this happen a couple of times.

It was always an exciting place to be. Women coming and going all day long and it always amazed me that people could come in the door in one mood and leave in a completely different mood. As soon as they were sitting in my mom's chair they would tell her everything that is going on in their lives. There could be twenty people in that shop and the other hairdressers working their magic all buzzing around and laughing and talking. But when my mom had someone in her chair, it seemed like there was a bubble around them. Snip, snip my mom's scissors would click and snip and the transformation would happen. My mom probably knew more about everyone in our town than anyone else.

I asked her why people always told her their secrets. She said that it was because she worked with their crown chakra. For a long time, I thought she said "clown chocolate" and could not figure out where the clown was or where the chocolate was hidden. Did she put it in the beehive?

Anyway, I never forgot her telling me about that but we never really discussed it anymore. One day, I had a bad day when I first started high school. I tried out for the basketball team and didn't make it. I didn't even want to try out but my dad made me.

I was more nervous about telling him than anything else because just that morning he told me that I was going to get into sports and get my head out of the books for a while. I was upset and my eyes were a little red and I decided to walk over to the beauty shop to see her. When I walked in I asked her if she had any of that clown chocolate to make me feel better.

She was doing somebody's hair and quickly put her scissors down and pulled me in the back room where she kept all the perm solution. She stared at me really hard and said "what did you say?"

My eyes were watering a little bit because I was trying not to cry and I told her that I just needed some clown chocolate., 'cause I was having a bad day. Then she said "what kind of drugs did you take?" Was it pot? Pills?! TELL ME RIGHT NOW!"

Then she went on this tirade about high school being too grown up right now and I was associating with the wrong crowd and I needed to find some different friends because she was not going to have a pothead daughter running around and talking about clowns and chocolate and not making any sense.

"My God" she screamed! " You are the oldest! You are setting the example for your sister and brother!"

It was times like these when she reminded me so much of Aunt Darcy. They could both fly off the handle and go on these rants and you wouldn't even know what set them off. When she ran out of breath, she said "I'm going to ask you one more time. What. Kind. Of. Drugs. Did .YOU. TAKE!"

I let loose with my own tirade. I started bawling like a baby and told her about the basketball team and what dad said that morning and then told her "I don't know why dad made me try out because I hate basketball!! And if you don't want me to have the clown chocolate, then you should just say so. Give it all to your customers!" "And," I screamed at her "I am sick and tired of always being the oldest!"

Well, she calmed down a little and asked me to explain what I was talking about. I reminded her of when I asked her why people came in to the beauty shop in a bad mood and then left in a good mood and she told me it was because she worked with the clown chocolate.

She looked confused for a minute and then it dawned on her what I was talking about. She started grinning, then it turned in to one of those laughs that comes out in spurts. She took a deep breath then belly laughed. She actually laughed so hard that she had to cross her legs so she wouldn't pee herself.

She said "Do you mean the crown chakra?" "because that is what I said, not the clown chocolate."

I just stared at her for a minute, "I guess so."

"Ok Sis, the crown chakra is something the Orientals call the top of the head. They do some sort of medicine or meditation on it and it makes people feel better. I only said that because I work with people's heads and that is where the crown chakra is."

"Oh, I guess I was confused a little then. Mom, I don't do pot. I don't even know where to get it. And neither do my friends."

"Well," she said, "I am glad about that."
"Don't worry about telling your dad about the basketball team. I will tell him and you don't ever have to try out for anything you hate anymore.

My dad works for the City. He does all kinds of work like keeping roads built and the water running. He is usually really tired when he comes home from work. So, when he does come in he expects me to have the tea made and the koolaid ready for the kids for supper. I am the one to do it because I am the oldest and the only one allowed to operate the stove whenever they are not home. I also get to do the cooking when mom has to work late at the beauty shop.

My dad loves things like birds and aquariums. He has two 55 gallon aquariums sitting in the living room and has had the same fish in there forever. His favorite fish was this big sucker fish that he got when it was little, but over the years it has grown up so much that dad had to get the big aquariums.

He also likes for things to be the same and normal everyday so that he knows what to expect. His rules are pretty simple. "Mind him or else." The "or else" is the belt, and he is not afraid to use it.

In our family, things are never normal so he spends a lot of time with the aquariums and the

Men's Feet Pie

birds. It helps to keep him calm, always messing around with the birds or the fish.

Saturday was the day that he was not to be interrupted for anything, because that is when ABC's Wide World of Sports came on.

It was always started the same way. First, that music would play and that was dad and Willie's signal that it was on. Then, Willie would announce right along with the opening intro.

"Spanning the Globe to bring you the constant variety of sports.
The thrill of victory…
the agony of defeat…
the human drama of athletic competition..
This is ABC's Wide World of Sports."

Then they would both plop down and start their sports program. Even though I didn't care for sports, I always had to watch that introduction. I had seen it a hundred times, but I always cringed and gritted my teeth whenever that poor skier went crashing down the ski ramp…the agony of defeat……. After seeing that, I went on about my day.

We were fortunate in my family. We had two television sets. One was for the whole family, and in the living room, and the other one was in the back room with the card table, and was really only used for watching ballgames and the news. The one in the living room was for things like the Brady Bunch, Gilligans Island, and Little House on the Prairie. The line up on tv was always the same after we got home from school. Then, it was outside to play until supper. Most of the time, we went out and played after supper until the streetlights came on, but we did have other shows that we watched all the time too. We had three channels.

The TV in the living room was this big wooden box and on top of it was where we kept the tv guide. That was always kept out of Willie's reach. Every week during grocery shopping was when we would get the new TV guide and Willie would get the old one to color in.

No one ever caught him doing it, but somehow Willie would take all the knobs off the TV's. The real mystery is that no one knew where he put them and he wasn't telling. The Sears repair man had to come over to the house so much to replace them and finally, Dad just attached a pair of vice grips to all of the knobs and that is what we use to change channels.

Willie had this thing about commercials. He loved them almost as much as I loved my books. He would be playing in the floor with his toys, and when one of his commercials came on, he would stop whatever he was doing and immediately begin talking. He could mimic every word.

Willie's favorite day was Cartoon Day. He would fly out of bed first thing in the morning wearing nothing but his Superman Underoos and grab a towel that he clipped together with a clothes pin to wear as a cape. Then, to the kitchen for his bowl and cereal and off to the living room.

On Saturday we always had some cousins over. Bryn and Zack were always there and occasionally others would show up. We just called it Cartoon day and that is when all the adults just left the kids alone in the living room to watch TV. Nobody left the living room unless it was to get some more cereal.

Willie and Zack would just sit there eating their cereal and then when a good commercial came on they would talk right along with it and pretend that they were in the commercial. But, when Schoolhouse Rock came on, they would go a little out of control singing and dancing with it until it was over. Little Zack would start out with "Conjunction junction, what's your function?" and Willie would answer "Hooking up words and phrases and clauses."

Then they would have this back and forth sing along with each of them doing their part. Nobody would dare interrupt them while they were in the middle of a Schoolhouse Rock song. One time, our little cousin Jimmy had come over and thought that he was going to interrupt the singing by acting silly and pretending to change the channel. Willie and Zack were right in the middle of performing "I'm just a Bill, I'm only a Bill....Sitting here on Capitol Hill......" He got punched right in the nose by Willie, who never missed a beat of the song. They were crazy about those songs.

Then after the cartoons were over, at about noon, everybody would clean up the Saturday morning mess in the living room and go on with the rest of the day. Usually, Dad would come home from work at about that time and start getting stuff together for the afternoon Wild World of Sports.

Saturdays were the best day during the week. Cartoons in the morning, play all afternoon with the kids in the neighborhood, or go to some family dinner. During the summers, we also got to stay up late watching tv until the National Anthem played before TV programming went off. After that song was over, the tv would get all fuzzy with lines and it was time to get in to bed.

IMMACULATE CONCEPTION

     I gassed up the Cutlass Supreme again just before I left Colorado and hit the Kansas State Line. Another call to my dad to let him know where I was on the road and the same list of instructions from him and I was on my way. He wanted to let me know that he was watching the weather and I might run into some snow and if it got too bad, I needed to pull over. It had been snowing a little but nothing major. Just as I pull out on to the highway, I see them. The Snow Snakes. It seems as if every pivotal moment in my life has involved snow snakes. Most people don't call them snow snakes, but a lot of people have experienced them.
     Snow snakes happen when you are driving down a highway when it is bitterly cold outside and there has been a light snow recently. The conditions have to be absolutely perfect, and when they occur, the snow forms into these long twisty

ropes of air and snow. Then the slightest wind will have snow snakes dancing, swirling, and undulating across the road. The effect can be mesmerizing, but can be quite dangerous if you are watching them for hours on end while amped up on caffeine and dreading the end of your journey. It seems like nearly everything important in my life has happened during a time where I see this weird and strange dance of snow and air.

Kansas is windy, and the snow snakes were really crazy looking. Then it started to snow really hard. I was cussing earlier because it was so cold, but with the wind and the snow acting up, I thought I better stop with the cussing and start in with the praying.

There are a lot of stories in my family, but now is not the time to go into them. I need to concentrate on the road, because I tend to daydream and let my mind wander when I am driving. I sure don't want to have a wreck. So, I drive down that highway looking out for black ice and watch all of the snow snakes and then the snow really started flying.

Even though it was daylight, I felt like I was in outer space with the way the snow was coming at me. I was a little scared so I start in on The Lord's Prayer, which is one of the first things I learned in Catholic School.

My family was not Catholic. Some of the Aunts went to the Baptist Church, but we did not have one church that we all went to. I didn't start out at the Immaculate Conception but went to the regular school. My first day there, I made some new friends and one of them was a boy and he kissed me. I told mom all about it when I went home that day and the next thing I knew, I was changing schools. I could hear my mom and dad arguing about it that night. My dad said that he was not going to allow his baby to get kissed at school and he was sure that the nuns didn't allow that crap to happen.

  The first time I stepped in to the Church, it took my breath away. The entire school had walked over from the schoolhouse in single file by grade. Before walking through the big wooden doors , I could smell the incense. When we walked in to the entry that was just like a little room, the other kids stuck their hands in a bowl of water and made the sign of the cross. The stained glass seemed to me alive, with all of those pictures.

  The sunlight was streaming through the stained glass windows and painted the entire side of the church and all of the pews with its colors. People were painted and so were the pews. I looked at my arms and right there was Jesus and Mary on my skin. I opened and closed my hand just to see if I could capture a little bit of Jesus. Mary looked so sad that I lightly touched her with my other hand, trying to wipe her tears away. I knew all about Jesus, and I knew that Mary was the Mother of God, but I had no idea that she was so sad and beautiful.

  I did not know at the time that it was Mary, but I knew that she must be very important to be right there in the windows with Jesus. I felt my eyes well up and my chest started to hurt with the sadness of it all. It seemed like my ears opened up too because I heard the most amazing singing but only by one voice.

The priest, Father Aloyisious, was chanting a song in Latin. I didn't know that it was Latin until later. I thought that must be how angels and God and Mary and Jesus all speak to each other, in that mysterious chanting language. It made the hair on the back of my neck stand up.

With my chest filling up and my ears open really wide, I looked around that painted church and felt like I belonged. It was like I was being hugged by giant soft arms. I never wanted to leave. Just when I thought I couldn't take it anymore of this peaceful feeling without drifting right up to Heaven, I got a painful smack right on the top of my head. The ears that were listening for more of that Angel Language got pulled practically right outta my head when Sister Bridget yanked me over to a pew.

She muttered under her breath…"heathen, Don't even know how to act in God's House. Don't play with your hands, you fold them in prayer and ask God to forgive you."

I sat in my pew and tried to be pious, and while Sister Bridget was hitting someone else, I opened my hands once more and captured a little bit of Jesus from the sunlight on the stained glass windows. I could not see him on my hands anymore when we left the church, but I felt like He stayed with me all day long.

The Catholic School I went to was small. There were 90 students in the whole school, and that included grades 1 through 8. We had our routines every day at school. No matter whether

Sister Bridget was in a good mood, or a bad mood, we always did the same thing. It started first thing.

For eight years of Immaculate Conception, the days of the week were always the same. Up at 7 am, then cinnamon toast and milk for breakfast. Getting ready for school was easy because we wore the same uniform every single day. Plaid jumper with a white shirt that had iron creases up the sleeve. In the winter, we could wear a dark blue sweater vest over that. White bobby socks turned down and the final touch to getting ready was black and white saddle oxfords. If it was warm, we walked to school, but if it was raining or cold out, Mom would load us all up into the brown station wagon and drop us off in the schoolyard.

Everyone played as hard as they could until it was time to go in. If it was warm out, we would sit in the grass and make necklaces out of white clover flowers or swing on the playground. The bell was a big brass thing, with a wooden handle. Most of the younger ones could not even lift it, which is why the nuns waited until you were in fourth grade to get your turn to ring it.

Every week, a different student in the class was put in charge of leading the routines. The bell would ring, and we would go in and take our seats. Then, Sister Bridget would tell us who got to lead with the Lord's Prayer. After the prayer, we would say the Pledge of Allegiance standing, with our hands over our hearts. Every grade did the same thing. Then, we would start on our lessons. Since the school was so small, two grades were in one classroom with each other. Sister Bridget was the first and second grade teacher. Then we would go on to the next teacher in the next two grades. But, as luck would have it, Sister Bridget moved up to teach the third and fourth grade just when I moved up.

Studies were usually interesting. I always loved history and art the best. At lunchtime, one of the 7th or 8th graders would ring the bell and then it was off to the Grill for those good grilled cheese sandwiches and some sweet tea. On Wednesday, we always went to mass at noon. Every afternoon, we had Religion, where we learned how to be "good Catholics."

That was when Father Aloysious would come over and teach the class. He basically told us stories and parables. But he also made us learn all of the books of the Bible and Chapters. We memorized them at first by learning them in a song, and then we could recite them without singing. Life was usually pretty good at school, you knew what to expect and you also knew what you could get away with (which was practically nothing).

Sister Bridget had her long yardstick, but all of the other teachers had something too. Sister Mary had a slim wooden paddle and Sister Amelia had a fat paddle with holes drilled in to it. And none of them were afraid to use it. We were all terrified that they would use it on one of us.

It was not so much that it hurt (which it did), but the shame of it. Because they wouldn't take you out in to the hallway, they did it in front of everyone in the class. Sister Amelia would always say the same thing if someone was going to get it.

She would say the person's name and then yell FRONT AND CENTER!

Everybody in class would stop what they were doing and sit up straight in their chairs. If they weren't in their chairs, they would get there quick. "Front and Center" meant that you walked to the front of the room, right in the center of her desk. Then she would tell you how many licks you were getting and to grab the desk. You would bend over, with your back end facing the whole world, and then you would get the licks.

After it was done, she would hand you the paddle so that you could go hang it back up on the wall right behind her desk. Then, with your head hung, you walked back to your seat and nobody would look at you. It would usually take about a week for the shame to leave and things get back to normal for most of us. But not Joey O'Dell. He didn't care if he got paddled every single day. He would get it, then practically skip back to his seat.

It was almost like he expected to get in trouble all the time, so he did. The only time he cried was when he had to get his licks from Father Aloyisious. Father hit him so hard that he would go airborne for just a minute. After his first paddling from Father Al, he changed his ways. Because if he got stirred up and acted like he was going to cause trouble, the nuns would just have to say to him,. You don't want me to call Father Al back to the school? Do you?
Catholic school didn't have a lunch room. A lot of kids brought a sack lunch, but there was a small group of kids that would walk to the grill every day

for lunch. After the lunch bell rang, we walked around the courthouse and across the square to a little hole-in-the wall restaurant called The Grill. The best cheeseburgers in the state. Of course everyone had their favorite meal.

The owners of the Grill did not want the dining room full of kids eating, because there were only about 12 tables in the whole restaurant and of course the counter. Those important seats were for lawyers and courthouse people, and the occasional farmer. So they had a special place reserved for us every day at lunch in the kitchen, right next to the griddle and the deep fryer. It was a big round table and seated about ten kids comfortably. Everybody at school took lunch at the same time. We would all file in and take our seats.

We were all dressed in plaid uniforms and it looked like some sort of Scottish ceremony the way we all walked in single file. After the first week of school, they knew what we all drank and usually had our drinks ready. They usually knew what we were going to eat too. The fare was simple. Burgers, fries, and grilled cheese sandwiches. The way they served the grilled cheese sandwiches was sliced diagonally, with a pile of sliced dill pickles right on top of the sandwich in the middle. So, you could dip your grilled cheese in the pickle juice and then take a bite, and then top it off with a fry and take a big slurp of good sweet tea. The flavors mixed perfectly.

I would imagine that the cook at the grill knew more about Sister Bridget than all of the parents and other teachers. She was usually the topic of conversation around the table. For some reason, we all felt comfortable there. Between us and the rest of the world were the swinging doors that separated the kitchen from the dining room. All we could hear was the sizzle and pop from the giant griddle and the occasional laughter of the waitress. Mrs. Rosie was the main cook and she was like a lot of our Grandmas. If we acted up or didn't have good manners, she would get us. We also knew that if we did not act right she had no problems smacking someone with a spatula.

But the conversation always turned to Sister Bridget and who she was mad at that day. Maria was my best friend and she hated Sister Bridget. With good reason. Sister Bridget was always yelling at Maria, but she could never make her cry. Then, Maria would do something to get back at her, but would hardly ever get caught. I always admired that about Maria, even though it made me nervous.

One time I got especially nervous when we went to Mass on Wednesday like we always did. Maria had just popped in a mouthful of Bazooka gum so that she could see the comic and was chewing away on the walk over from the school. We had just entered the church when Sister Bridget said

"Maria! Are you chewing gum in the Lord's House?"

Smooth as could be, Maria put her fingers in her mouth and got that gum out just as Sister Bridget walked up to her. She made Maria open her mouth and show her and then said "go on.

She watched as Maria walked up to the Holy Water and dipped her fingers in to make the sign of the cross. I was shaking, because I saw the Bazooka gum on the tips of Maria's fingers dip right in to that Holy Water and I fully expected the church to go up in flames or for Maria to turn to stone right there.

Who ever heard of putting Bazooka gum in Holy Water. Maria started to laugh when she saw me and then snorted because she was trying to hold it in. I couldn't help but laugh and then we felt the hot glare from Sister Bridget so we both acted like we were coughing because of the incense.

Sister Bridget was a small woman. We never knew what color her hair was because she always wore the habit. I always imagined it to be a mousy brown with a long gray streak in it. A streak of meanness. She had a hooked nose, small hands and she almost never smiled. When she did, she could appear to be nice, but you had to watch the smile to see if she showed teeth or if her mouth was closed. If she smiled that way, you knew that she was gritting her teeth and some body was gonna get it.

I used to "get it" in first grade every time I tried to write something down because I used the wrong hand. She hated it whenever someone wrote or drew with their left hand. As soon as I picked up the pencil, she would whack the back of my hand with that yardstick and glare at me. She would make this big show of snatching up the pencil that I just dropped and put it in to my right hand. Then she would whack my right hand if the letters weren't perfect. I hated it when she did that.

We did not think that any of the other nuns liked Sister Bridget, because whenever they talked to her they always had their lips pursed, and their noses wrinkled like something smelled bad. I was in fifth grade when I had endured long years of Sister Bridget. She took the joy out of learning and made it seem like a chore. And that you were an awful person just for daring to exist.

Finally, she left. She got transferred to somewhere else. Probably to New York. She always talked about New York like it was some magical place that none of us would ever go to, kind of like Heaven. We were all shocked and wanted to feel liberated, but there was a possibility that whoever replaced her would be even worse. Up until that time, we all prayed that she would leave. But when it happened, we were almost wishing to keep the devil that we knew than have to face someone else.

But then, we got Sister Joan. She immediately earned the attention and even love of every one of the students. Now, in some ways she was even tougher than Sister Bridget. When it came to spelling, she insisted that we knew how to spell our words of the week, and how to use them in a sentence. It's kind of funny, that Sister Bridget would only give us ten words a week, and we all struggled with getting the spelling just right.

Sister Joan gave us twenty words a week, and not only did we have to take a spelling test every Friday, we had to turn in our creative writing project using every single one of the words on our list. Now, that was a challenge. She gave each one of us a dictionary and we had to use the words correctly and make the story we wrote fun to read. She gave out two awards every Monday. One for the best penmanship, and one for the most creative. I got the award for most creative a lot. I never got the award for penmanship.

She always wrote on my papers, "great story, but it looks like a chicken wrote it." I never understood what she meant by that until one day when I asked her if she really thought I looked like a chicken. I was almost in tears and she looked shocked and then busted out laughing.

She explained that it was a phrase that meant something else. When people called bad writing chicken scratch, because it looks all scraggly and not neat and lined up.

I started crying even harder but then stopped when she told me that most of the famous writers in the world wrote that way and that I had so much creativity in me that I didn't pay attention to things like making a perfect letter. And that she would not have me any other way.

"Anyway, you will learn to type soon and that will take care of your chicken scratch, but you will still be creative."

I loved her even more then, and couldn't wait to learn to type. She also told me that if I tried, she believed that I might actually become a famous writer myself.

Before Sister Joan, it would be whack, whack with the ruler on your head if you miss-spelled a word. Sister Joan had a lot of fun with us and it made us want to learn. If you miss-spelled a word, sister Joan would take time out with you and spell the word over and over again and kind of make it rhyme and sometimes, she would even put the word to music and make us make up a song by spelling the word correctly and using it in a phrase. Pretty soon, all of us got much better with our spelling.

     Before Sister Joan, none of us liked to spell, but we liked getting whacked with that ruler even less. The best thing about getting your paper back from Sister Joan was the things that she wrote on it. She wrote with a red ink, but she made big swirly letters and even drew happy or sad faces on your paper. No matter how bad your paper was, she always made you feel good. If you made a mistake, she helped you figure out how to fix it instead of grabbing that ruler.

     Sister Joan loved plays and music. She sang all the time, and played the guitar. And it wasn't just the church songs either. She would give us an assignment of writing a play, then we would have to put together the cast and act it out in front of the whole class. Another thing she did was put on talent shows.

     The best ones were when she had us act like we were on the Gong Show with Chuck Berry. One of the older boys usually pretended to be Chuck Berry and host the show. And there were always three judges that had the gong. We usually did this once a month. My best friend Maria and I would put together an act to see if we could win. We always did songs. I thought Maria was going to beat up Kurt Rich the time he got to act like Chuck Berry. We had put together this great song act where we sang with the cassette player one of our favorite songs. It was called Afternoon Delight by the Starlight Vocal Band. We had wrapped some deodorant bottles in aluminum foil so that they would look like singing mikes and had this dance routine all worked up.

Well, we started the cassette and went into our dance with Maria starting out and me doing the part of harmony in the background. I looked up and saw all the nuns standing there with frowns on their faces when I was singing the part "Skyrockets in flight.....Afternoon Delight."

I knew that meant some kind of trouble and that is when Kurt walked over and hit the gong three times by himself without the judges doing anything. Then he tried to be funny and said really loud that he thought we should be wearing the deodorant instead of singing in to it.

Maria was really into the song by then and could not believe that we got gonged, but when Kurt said what he did, she turned red. The mad kind of red, not the embarrassed kind.

She whispered to him when she walked by that she was going to "get him" after school. Kurt wised up and knew that she would. Maria could get a little crazy and wasn't afraid to fight a boy as long as no adult knew about it.

Sister Joan did not wear a habit. And I knew that there was definitely something different about her when I saw her at the carnival. There was a group of old men that sat on the corner right on

Men's Feet Pie

Main Street. Nobody knew where they lived, because they could be seen on that corner at almost any time of the day or night. They always had a brown paper bag and they passed it back and forth between them . They were dirty, had long beards, and smelled bad. One of them always had a snotty nose and it always grossed me out and I wondered why he did not have a Kleenex. These men were always on that corner and did not move for parades, carnivals, or funeral processions. They were known to everyone in town as The Bums and people generally cut a wide path around them. Not Sister Joan. She would go right up and talk to them.

The carnival came to town every year in the fall. We would have the Saturday parade and the carnival for four nights. Well, it was time for the Saturday Parade and everyone in town was there. As I was walking down the street with my friends, I looked over and there was Sister Joan, sitting on the curb with the bums and they were talking to her and laughing and then one of the bums passed the paper bag to Sister Joan and she smiled and said thanks, and then took a swig herself. We all gasped, and stood there in shock because Sister Joan was sharing a drink with the snotty man and the other bums.

She was wearing jeans and a sweat shirt and looked just like everybody else there. We did not know what to think of our Sister Joan then. But a funny thing that happened after that.

Some of the parents walked up to say something mean to Sister Joan about her behavior on Main Street but she did not even give them a chance. She smiled and started introducing everyone to the bums, and even called them by name. After that, when we were circling town, they were not the bums any more. They were Clay, Earnest, and Richard. People would even say hello to them if they were walking down the street.

My respect for Sister Joan was so great, that I thought that she would magically turn those men in to upstanding citizens. That they would become decent men and get jobs and get off that corner. I don't think any of them ever got off the corner, but that didn't seem to matter much to Sister Joan.

Sister Joan changed something else for us too. Once a year, scholastic book fair came around. That first sheet of papers that showed all the books you could buy. I would stare for hours at that sheet and could never pick out just a book or two. I wanted them all. Mom would get me books and Grandma always wanted to look over what I picked out. That is how I got all of the Nancy Drew and Hardy Boys books. It did not take long to collect the whole sets of both series because I also got new books for my birthday and usually there was one in my Easter basket.

The only series that I really loved more than the Little House Books was the Trixie Belden Books and Sister Joan made sure to point them all out to me on the sheet so that we could order them.

IRENE

Enough about Catholic School. I guess the praying has paid off, because the snow stopped coming down, even thought it was still all over the road and making snow snakes.

I remember the first time I really saw them. The Snow Snakes. I must have been 8or 9 years old and I got to go on a trip to pick up Uncle Jake. We were coming back from St Louis.

Mom and Dad borrowed Grandpa's Pink Pontiac so that they could pick Uncle Jake up and bring him home for Thanksgiving. He had moved up there for a job in the pretzel factory and stayed with one of my Grandma's brothers for a couple of years. So we were all excited that he was going to come back home to live.

He had to move to St. Louis to get out of town for a while because he got into trouble with the law. Grandma thought it best for him to get away until things calmed down. He didn't really do anything bad except to get into a car with a bunch of his friends who had all been out drinking that day.

Five minutes after getting in the car with them, the driver ran into the back of a parked police car. The policeman was knocked out and the boys in the front seat were hurt, so Uncle Jake got out of the car and decided to drive the police car in to town and get some help.

So, Uncle Jake pulled into the first place he saw, which was a bar and goes in to use the pay phone to call for an ambulance. He has the cop laying over in the front seat still passed out. He borrowed a quarter from an old guy sitting at the counter and makes the call and when he comes out of the bar to check on the cop, two other police men show up.

Uncle Jake was nervous and scared. He just graduated from high school and was still wearing his letter jacket, which was covered with blood. The cops see this and then look in the car and see the cop laid out in the front covered with blood and they pulled their guns and billy sticks and beat the crap out of Uncle Jake before he could even tell them what happened. They broke off one of his front teeth and gave him a busted lip.

Uncle Jake tried to fight the cops off of him while he was screaming about what happened. He was arrested for stealing a cop car and leaving the

Men's Feet Pie

scene of an accident. Then they said that he tried to resist arrest, which was ridiculous because he did not even know why they would arrest him when he was just going to get help. But, even though things were going to be ok, Uncle Jake had to go before the Judge and tell his side of the story.

My Grandma was so hot about this that it took all of her sons and Grandpa to hold her down and keep her from going to the police station that night. One thing about Grandma, she could not stand it when any of her kids were hurt, especially the boys. She told me once that girls were tougher than boys, especially in our family. Sometimes the women had to take care of the business.

So, she wanted to take care of this business that night but she had to wait until the next day to get him out of jail and go before the Judge. Everybody in the family went to the courthouse because we had heard that he was beat up pretty bad. Grandma had stayed up all night crying in a mad sort of way, but she pulled herself together before going in and told everybody that she was going to be able to stay calm. We all knew better.

We did not know what might happen, but one thing that we knew was that Grandma was not going to stay calm. I was about five and got to go and get dressed up for this. So, everybody in the family goes in and is really quiet until they bring Uncle Jake out of the back room to stand in front of the Judge. He was purple everywhere and one of his eyes was swollen shut and all bloody. Grandma started to shake and then the Judge called the court to order. He read off the charges against Uncle Jake and said "do you plead guilty or not guilty?" Uncle Jake said "NOT GUILTY, I WAS GOING FOR HELP" and that is when the Judge cut him off and said "all I need is a guilty or a not guilty, son, you will get your day in court."

That is when Grandma stood up and said that there was no need to go to court because he was innocent!!!!!" The Judge looked up and had this look on his face that was like he was better than everybody else and said "Ma'am, one more word out of you and I will hold you in contempt of court!" Grandma doesn't miss a beat and says "Well, that is fine because I don't have anything *but contempt for your court!"*

Everyone in the courtroom started laughing which really made the Judge mad and he said "I won't tell you again....SIT DOWN, or I will have you arrested. "

Grandma didn't sit. Instead she started yelling about Jake needing medical attention and who was gonna pay for that tooth, and didn't he know that Jake was a good boy just out having a good time…and she said a bunch more but that was while the deputies were carrying her out of the courtroom and booking her on disturbing the peace and contempt of court.

So, Grandma ended up in the cell just down the hall from Uncle Jake that night until everybody could get together enough money to post bail.

Getting bail money was not really hard to do, because once the story was out about what happened, a lot of people came by the house to pitch in. Grandma and Grandpa had helped out just about everyone in town at one time or another. Most of the people who came by were family members who had been in trouble at one time or another and Grandma either cooked them dinner or gave them a couch to lay on when they just needed a place to land for a while.

So, the bail was raised, and they both got out of jail and came home to figure out what to do and who to get for a lawyer. The lawyer was a good ole boy and said that he would be able to get all of the charges dropped and he did, except for the one of resisting arrest. Uncle Jake had to appear one more time to answer that charge and the morning of the trial all hell was breaking out at the house.

For one, I had fallen off the roof of Grandma's shed when I was trying to prove that I could fly. When I landed, I couldn't seem to get up and my leg hurt really bad. So, dad was yelling, he was another one who couldn't take it when somebody was hurt. He wanted to tear down the shed. Mom was trying to calm dad down and Grandma was in the kitchen ironing Uncle Jakes pants until she heard the ruckus with my mom and dad and me.

The dentist had given Uncle Jake a fake tooth to wear until he could get the real one fixed and while he was brushing his teeth, It fell down the drain, Grandpa and Uncle Lee were under the sink taking apart the pipes to find the tooth and Uncle Jake was yelling "forget the tooth!!" "If I am late they will put me in jail again and I am not going back in there." Every person in the house was yelling about something different and that is when

Grandma took charge.

She laid me on her bed and said that everything was going to be alright. She told Grandpa and Uncle Lee that they had to go to court with Uncle Jake and that it was probably better that the Judge did not see her face anyway. She might have to get arrested again and that would not do. Plus, the baby was hurt and she had to go to the hospital with me and my mom because my dad couldn't handle hospitals.

So, off we went, my mom holding me and my Grandma driving the 30 miles to the hospital. Grandma put on the radio and we listened to Elvis Presley. Grandma loved Elvis more than any other singer. She knew all of the songs by heart and sang them just like she was up on the stage with Elvis. My mom and Grandma sang out loud to help keep me calm until we got there and I got my first cast.

Anyway, the important thing was that Uncle Jake got to come home and we were all so happy. He was the first one to point out the snow snakes to me on the way home from St. Louis. We watched them dancing on the highway the whole way home. My sister was with us on that trip and stood up in the front seat in the middle of mom and dad and pointed them all out to me and Uncle Jake.

When we got home, there was a big dinner at Grandma and Grandpa's house to celebrate. Grandma had cooked his favorite, which was a roast with potatoes and carrots and lots of onions. The gravy was Uncle Jake's favorite, and he must have torn up a whole loaf of Wonder Bread to soak that gravy up. Grandma always liked to watch everybody eat. She was usually tired from all the cooking and would stand over at the counter and drink some sweet tea and say "go on…eat it all up. I have been sampling all day and I'm not even hungry right now." So we ate.

Uncle Jake was a little nervous about running into those cops again that beat him up so bad. One night, the first week he was home, he went circling town with some of his friends. Sure enough, they were pulled over. But the cop surprised them all and said "Jake, I bet your momma is glad to have you back. They are still telling stories about her at the jail." Then he laughed about it and "called her a tough old bird."

Jake wasn't sure what to think about this then the cop said "if you are looking for a job, I hear the funeral home is hiring. They need somebody to usher people for funerals and do some work around the place. If you are interested, go on in and tell 'em I sent you."

With that, the cop told them all to be careful and went on about his night.

So, the next morning, Uncle Jake borrowed a suit from Grandpa, who had only one, and went down to the funeral home to see if he could get some work. He wasn't too sure about working around dead people, but he needed the money. He got the job and started the next weekend. Uncle Jake took his job seriously and decided to be the best usher he could and was somber when he passed out the announcements and even held the hand of old ladies to escort them down the aisle to view the body. He worked his way up and before we knew it, he was driving the hearse, and leading the procession to the cemetery whenever somebody died. There was one particular funeral that changed all of our lives, even though we didn't know the person who died. It was at that funeral that Uncle Jake met Irene.

All of the uncles were married and had kids, except for Uncle Jake. And all of their wives had something about them that Grandma did not like.

You see, there was something in the men that made them all like their women a little on the crazy side. A nice, clean, boring woman just wouldn't do. It may have something to do with the fact that all of the men were stable and usually sane and had common sense. So, our family gatherings were always interesting, not because of the men, but because you never knew what was going to happen with the women.

Grandma didn't like any of her daughters-in-law. But she said several times that she knew that the men in the family couldn't help it. They got that part of their personality from Grandpa. (She never commented on the fact that Grandpa liked his women a little crazy too, and what did that say about her?) Anyway, we all adjusted to whoever was in the house and whatever their mood was and got along for the most part. Everybody knew that Grandma was the boss and as long as she was respected, there was not a problem. That was, until Uncle Jake brought Irene home.

Irene was one of those women that brought the crazy out in a man. She wore big hoop earrings, and her lips were big and red and looked juicy.

Her hair was all teased up and she always looked like she just came in from a wind storm, you know, breezy and breathless. She did this really weird thing with her eyebrows. She shaved them off, then drew eyebrows on. If you were up close you could really tell, 'cause the drawn on brows were higher than the shaved ones. Even the most calm and steady man could not keep their head about them when they dated her.

I don't know if it was the juicy red lips or the drawn on eyebrows, or a combination, but something about her made men go wild and made all the women hate her. They all called her the floozy whenever she was not in the room. And when she was in the room, they never called her by name.

I could not believe that Grandma let them get away with that, because it was bad manners to not call someone by name. Grandma didn't even insist that the kids call her Miss Irene, she let them get away with calling her "Uncle Jake's girlfriend." It was like she could not stand to here that name coming out of a grandbaby's mouth. Irene had something called a "reputation."

Maria told me that one of her cousin's dated her and that she "put out and then left him high and dry." I didn't know what "put out" meant but Maria told me, she was worldly like that.

Uncle Jake came home from St. Louis after the trouble with the law and settled down. He had a steady job working at the funeral home and was now the main guy down there. He wore suits to work every day and even thought he was only 27, he was treated right whenever he was out in town, really respectful. But when he got with Irene, he lost it a little.

In the beginning, it was small stuff. Like pacing the floor if she said that she was gonna go to the store and pick something up. He would pace the floor until she got back. If a friend of the family stopped by, which happened all the time, he would make sure that he was standing right beside her and always have a hand touching her, or would make sure to kiss her and be sure that the other guy saw it.

It was like he was marking his territory or something, the way dogs do. In the beginning, Irene ate it up. She would smile and flirt with Uncle Jake in front of everybody and kiss at the table, which really set grandma off. She thought it was bad manners and told Uncle Jake that the kids did not need to have their supper with the floozy acting up at the table.

We all knew from an early age what you could not do at the table. Loud crunching of food was even worse that talking with your mouth full, and talking with your mouth full would get you smacked and sent away from the table. Irene did all of those things.

Irene did a lot of things that upset the women in the family. For one, she acted like all of us kids were dirty. She never spoke to us unless she was getting on to us for something. A lot of people in the family smoked, but Irene had this really bad habit of putting her cigarette out in a coffee cup, or in one of the saucers. My mom hated that about her. What really set grandma off though was the

Men's Feet Pie

fact that Irene smacked her lips when she ate.

Now, in our family, certain things were expected of everyone, especially the kids. And that was good table manners. Anyone who smacked, chewed with their mouth open, or tried to speak with a mouth full of food was banned from the table until we could "act right."

So, you learned quickly that if you wanted to eat all that good food, you learned your manners, and it started when you were a baby. And it did not matter if your hair was straight or curly, you would have good table manners. So, Irene not only smacked, she moaned and groaned whenever she took a bite of something. The men would stare at her in fascination, especially when it came to Irene eating something sweet, because she would really "act up" with her moaning and licking of sweet icing off her lips. She knew she was center stage for the men.

So, all of the women in the family put up with her until she committed the ultimate act of bad manners at the table.

We were all just getting into the kitchen and Zack wanted to say the prayer. So, about twenty of us were standing there until everyone got quiet so that 5 year old Zack could say the blessing. Irene had just taken a drink and sucked up a big bunch of ice and kind of held it in her mouth. So, finally it was quiet and Grandma said go ahead honey say your prayer. Zack took a deep breath and said "Oh Heavenly Father" and we heard *CRUNCH CRUNCH*….."Thank you for this food"…….. *CRUNCH CRUNCH CRUUUUNCH* …Zack's lips started to quiver and he looked at Grandma who was scowling at the floor "That we are about to receive." *CRUNCH CRUNCH*

By this time, the men even knew that there was going to be trouble because this was stepping way over the line of bad manners to crunch ice while one of the babies was saying a sweet prayer. Not only was it bad manners, it was sacrilegious. *Crunch Crunch Crunch*...Irene's jaws were grinding just like a cow eating corn. With everybody being so quiet, the crunching was so LOUD that it actually hurt my ears and made me want to throw something at her.

Zack was so thrown off that he couldn't even remember the food prayer that was one of the first things he learned to say. So he looked at Grandma who gave him a little nod and it was like she was saying go ahead, we aren't worried about you messing up the words right now.

Little Zack did the best he could under the circumstances.

After he finished, you could have heard a pin drop. Except that Irene was still crunching and didn't seem to know that anything was wrong. But we all knew. Knew without a doubt that the crazy woman was about to get it from Grandma.

We were waiting for yelling and screaming, but then Grandma just stared at her and started smiling this really slow smile. Uncle Jake got so nervous that he actually stopped breathing for a few minutes as he slowly walked over to Irene and said lets go outside and have a smoke.

Some people are so stupid.

She didn't realize that Uncle Jake was trying to save her. She thought that he was telling her what to do so she shrugged him off and said "I'm starving, why don't you go fix me a plate." Grandma said "I will fix your plate for you."

Uncle Jake started talking real fast and said "now Momma, I will do that, don't you worry yourself with that …we are going to fix a plate …"

Grandma just held up her hand and Jake shut up real quick. Everybody was staring and by this time, Irene finally wised up and knew that something was wrong. So Grandma goes over to the bucket that she always served ice in and picked up a big handful. She turned around and threw a piece at Irene and hit her right in the face. "You like ice so much!!???" "Here, have some more!!"

Grandma started chunking ice at Irene like she was a baseball pitcher. She even wound up her arm before a couple of throws. Every time she threw a piece of ice, she yelled out something that had been bothering her about Irene. She yelled about Irene putting her cigarettes out in the dishes and coffee cups. She yelled about her damned red lipstick staining all of the glasses.

Irene tried to duck, she was so shocked. Then she got mad and thought she was going to tell Grandma off.

Big mistake.

She started yelling that Grandma was nuts and who throws ice at a guest and that she was a grown woman and if she wanted to crunch ice she was going to. So grandma picks up the whole ice bucket and walked over to Irene and dumped the whole thing on to Irene's teased up head.

Some of it had melted, so Irene was drenched too. Grandma wasn't finished. She was in a frenzy by this point and ran over to the counter and picked up an entire coconut crème cake and smashed it in to Irene's face and said "go on!"

" Act up with your smacking and licking of icing. Eat this whole cake!"

Irene's eyebrows melted down her face with the cake icing and the water. All the women in the family were smirking. They had put up with her bad manners, watched her flirt with their men, and seen her be rude to their children. They had been waiting for this moment and knew that at some point, Grandma would take matters in to her own hands if Jake did not come to his senses.

Sometimes, the women have to protect the men in their lives. They all had their own grudges and when a couple of the men were going to step forward and stop Grandma, their wives stepped right in front of them and just glared at them. The men stared while the women drove Irene from the family.

Once, over at Aunt Darcy's, I saw a bunch of chickens attack a half a watermelon and have it demolished in a matter of minutes. There was nothing left except a few pieces of dirt-smeared rind left in the yard.

The women of the family did pretty much the same to Irene, except it was with words and chunks of ice. They literally drove her to the door and out on to the street. She was a mess with her mascara running and her teased up head flattened out and her clothes all wet. They only stopped when Uncle Jake started crying.

The men were embarrassed for him and looked the other way, but Grandma walked right up to him and said "son, this is for the best. You deserve somebody decent."

Aunt Darcy was standing there and said " she never had any manners, and someone who doesn't have manners doesn't care about other people's feelings. I'll bet she farts in bed too." She said it so softly that Uncle Jake just nodded his head.

He said "Yes, she does fart in bed but I never really minded." He said it so softly that we could barely hear him. It was pitiful and took some time before Jake would come around the family again, he was so shamed. A grown man crying is a sad thing to see. It really made me wonder about the power some women can have over a man. That day I wondered if he was crying over Irene, or crying over Grandma doing what he should have done a long time ago.

Any time Irene would see one of us in town, she would pretend that we weren't there. Even though we all felt sorry for Uncle Jake, we were glad that Irene was gone.

CHRISTMAS

I love snow. Driving through this snowy Kansas highway is making me think about Christmas and how it is always the best time of the year and also because it is my Grandma's favorite holiday.

Christmas is a big thing in our family. In fact, it is so big that when Christmas is over we start planning for the next Christmas. Christmas Eve is always at Grandma and Grandpa's house but Christmas day is held at whoever drew last year. Since everybody lived in the same town they used to fight over who was going to have Christmas day when they started getting married. Nobody ever fought about Christmas Eve. Aunt Marie tried to get Christmas Eve one year but when she mentioned it everybody just got real quiet and looked at her.

Grandpa never really said much and usually smiled all of the time but he stopped smiling when Aunt Marie said that. He looked at Grandma who got real white and kind of pinched her mouth together. Then he looked at his plate on the table and said real quiet like, "now Marie, you know better than that." Then he asked for some more sweet potatoes and that ended the conversation.

But, as for Christmas day, Grandma said that every year they would draw names to see who got Christmas next year.

Christmas really got started the day after Thanksgiving. There were two things that happened to remind us that Christmas was on the way. It was the real beginning of the Holidays whenever the Sears Wish Book came in the mail and then the day after Thanksgiving, Mom would break out the Big Red Book.

Now the Sears Wish Book changed every year. We would sit for hours and hours flipping turning the pages so slowly so that we wouldn't miss a thing. That catalog of wishes was treated with an almost reverence by all the kids in the family. It would come in the mail so pretty and pristine with all the shiny and colorful pages and within a week the pages would be turned down, and dog eared from the constant use. If there was something that we really wanted, the pages would be rumpled and the corner turned down twice. It was bad manners to come right out and ask for something, unless, of course, a stranger or friend of the family asked you what you wanted Santa to bring to you. But to ask your parents was not considered really polite, but it was certainly within the rules to give hints.

The Big Red Book was the same one that

Mom pulled out every year. The real name of it was The Readers Digest Book of Christmas, but we just called it the Big Red Book. That the best part of Christmas for me and I looked forward to that book coming out more than anything.

It had a hard cover and was bigger than the Wishbook. Inside those pages were all of the stories about Christmas. The first page that you opened to was "Twas the Night Before Christmas." There were beautiful old timey pictures of Santas from around the world, pictures of food and even some favorite recipes. There were poems and paintings, and little facts about the holiday. Each page was illustrated with pictures of wooden toys, and spruce and holly.

I think I liked it because the pictures were all old timey. Like from centuries ago and it made me feel like I could go to Christmas in a lot of far-away places. My favorite pictures were of snow covered hills, with a big horse pulling a wagon with a Christmas tree, heading toward a village of people wearing capes and caps and tall snow covered boots.

The best thing to do was to sit on the couch looking at those two books and eating out of the glass bowl that always had the Christmas Candy in it. That was another thing that happened after Thanksgiving. Grandma had these glass bowls with lids that she filled with Christmas ribbon candy. We also set out the tins that had different kinds of hard candy with designs in the center.

She had another wooden bowl that she filled with the Brachs chewy candy in the wrappers.

There were all kinds of flavors of that candy. Grandma would load up a bunch of us kids and take us to the drug store and give us each a paper sack to fill up with candy. It was ok to leave it uncovered because all the pieces had a wrapper, and also because it looked pretty in the wooden bowl.

That time of year also had a certain smell. The spices of Christmas always changed the mood of everyone. The day after Thanksgiving Grandma would make the special tea that was made with Tang and instant tea and cinnamon and other good secret spices. She would make up big batches of the magic powder and put it in mason canning jars and give it out to everybody in the family. You could either have it hot or cold, and my favorite way was hot. It scented the whole house whenever you made a cup.

Every year, Grandma would be at the counter making the Christmas drink and all of the grandkids and some cousins would sit at the table putting cloves into oranges that we hung all over the house. That was the day that she put up her tree. Most people had a green tree, but not Grandma. Hers was a silver tinsel tree that would turn and play music. She had this big train set that she would let us set up under the tree that would go round and round. Usually, she would have to turn that train off because she would have so many presents piled up under it.

Each family had their own thing to make sure that you knew it was Christmas time. My mom loved Nativity scenes. She had one made out of white porcelain that sat on top of the piano and you saw it as soon as you came into our house.

Aunt Darcy loved Santa Clauses, and she had about a hundred of them scattered all over her house. And she didn't mind if the cats climbed all over them.

The food of Christmas was really something, because we had things that were not ever served at any other time. Grandma made homemade fruitcake that she sent to everyone in the family.

Big Tupperware bowls were filled with the different kinds of Christmas food. I'm sure that there was a proper name for the dishes, but we always called it "the red stuff," or "the green stuff," and everybody knew what we were talking about.

I remember most all of the Christmas times we had when we were kids, but there is one Christmas that I will never forget.

I was 12 and had just finished re-reading my prized collection of the Little House on the Prairie Books. I had every one of them, Grandma had given me all of the books at one time or another. I eventually wore out each of those books, and Grandma knew how much I loved them, so, last year for my birthday, she got me a boxed set of the books. The covers all matched and they fit into this neat collector's box all lined up perfectly. I finished Farmer Boy, for about the fourth time, on Christmas Eve and put it under my pillow. It was my favorite book out of the whole collection. It was the one that told about Almanzo Wilder and his time growing up. The next morning, we all got up and opened our gifts and then got dressed and ready for all of the cousins to come over.

We cleaned our room and made the beds I tucked my book in just the way I liked it under my pillow.

I was in the kitchen helping cook and peel potatoes when I heard Bobbie Sue yelling. All of the grown-ups were outside looking at Mom's Christmas present. I followed the trouble and found the cousins in my bedroom jumping up and down on our beds.

My sister was yelling for them to get out, because she liked things neat and she also did not want anyone touching her new Christmas toys. She was 8 years old, and all of the cousins were afraid of her individually, but when they were in a group, they were like a pack of wild dogs and not afraid of anything (except maybe my dad). I went in to the room to stop what was going to turn into a bloody fight on Christmas Day just in time to see Bryn pick up Farmer Boy and throw it at my sister.

She saw me just as the book was leaving her hands and tried to hang on to it but only got a grip on the front cover. RIPPPP......

It was as if the world stopped turning and everything happened in slow motion. With the ripping off of the front cover, the binding came apart and the pages floated to the floor like leaves in a silent wind. All of the kids stopped in mid jump and kind of crumpled to the bed and slowly slid to the floor. Nobody was looking at me except Bryn, and she couldn't take her eyes off me. She started to cry.

There was not a sound to be heard in that

room. Five seconds ago, there was screaming, crying, hysterical laughter, and with the senseless act of violence towards my collector's copy of Little House, the reality changed. My sister just stared at me. She had never seen me really mad about anything, and she just did not know what I was going to do.

I had never felt that mad and did not know what I was going to do myself. I started to shake and just pointed towards the door. Everybody walked out in single file. Some of the younger kids paid their condolences on the way out... only in the way that little kids can.

First they would look at me and then look away, then little Zack grabbed me and hugged me so tight and said "sorry about your book..."then his face crumpled into a little cry and I felt better. I don't know why that made me feel better, but it did.

Somehow, the fact that somebody else, even if he was only five knew that I was so sad and wanted to let me know that he was sad for me, even though he didn't understand a thing about books and how important they were.

After the kids all left me alone, I collected myself and slowly picked up the pages. I found a big rubber band and put my book back together the best that I could and carefully put it in to place in the box. It wouldn't fit, but I gently coaxed it back in.

Then I put the whole box up on the top shelf in my closet so that nothing else could happen to my books. I dried my tears and said a prayer to Jesus to let me get through the day without crying

Men's Feet Pie

and without slugging Bryn.

I was 12 and too old to be telling on the kids and nobody would understand anyway. I was too old to beat Bryn up, and too young to spank her. I was also too old to go in front of a bunch of grownups and cry about my books. So, I practiced smiling a couple of times in front of the mirror and went back into the kitchen to finish those potatoes.

The grownups were all still outside looking at the new washer and dryer mom got from Santa, but the kids were in the kitchen. I rounded the corner just in time to hear Bryn, say

"MMMM that sure smells good. What is it?"

Zack, told her that Grandma called it Men's Feet Pie.

"Nu Unh" Said Bryn. "Grandma would not make a pie out of men's feet."

"Yeah she did," I heard Zack say. "She got up really early to grind all the stuff that goes in it and told me what it was called. "

"Well, this smells good and if it was out of men's feet it would stink. Plus there would be toenails in it and Grandma would never let toenails be in the food."

Zach huffed and said, "All I know is that Grandma called it Men's Feet Pie and you know that mom is going to make you eat it."

Now, I know that I had prayed to Jesus just a few minutes ago to let me get through the day, without crying and without slugging Bryn, and I trust in Him to help with that. But I never said anything about passing up a chance to get back just a little bit. In my sadness over losing my book, the thought of getting even with her had not occurred to me. But the opportunity presented itself and I like to think that Jesus did it on purpose.

I walked in to the kitchen real nonchalant like I didn't have a care in the world. I knew that the pie in the oven was Mincemeat pie, because I helped Grandma make the crust. But instead of letting the kids know what it was I said

"Boy, that Men's Feet Pie sure does smell good. I have to ask Uncle Jake who died at the funeral home this week."

Then I walked right by Bryn without even looking at her but I knew that she was trying not to cry. Bryn's mom made her try a bite of everything when we had family dinners. Even if she did not like the food, she had to at least put a piece in her mouth and swallow. It was just good manners.

So, I went back to peeling the potatoes and didn't have to pretend to smile because I knew that for the rest of the day Bryn would be thinking about eating a pie made out of stinky men's feet, and dreading dinner instead of looking forward to it. I had no idea how my little act of vengeance would affect that Christmas Day, and every Christmas after that.

My youngest brother, Willie, was about six that Christmas. He was so excited that he wasn't sick this year, because the year before, he had the stomach flu and threw up all Christmas Eve and Christmas Day. He remembered it because he threw up on all of his toys that were sitting in his pile. It is amazing that he remembered it, but it

Men's Feet Pie

must have been so traumatic for him to not get to play with his toys.

This Christmas, he wasn't sick, and he was getting on everybody's nerves because he was so hyper. Willie also loved to eat and dessert was his favorite thing after mashed potatoes. Well, the story had already got out about the pie. Bryn was on the verge of tears all day and whenever the subject of the food came up, she would start with the tears. Willie asked her what was wrong and when she told him about the pie, he turned really white in the face and said "I am not eating toes!"

" Maybe we should steal the pie and hide it outside or bury it or something."

The adults were all clueless about the conversation and did not know that one pie had 12 kids in a turmoil. Because everyone knew that somebody's mom would make them eat at least a bite. We got through dinner and sure enough, it was time for dessert. The kids all avoided looking at that pie and tried to pretend that they were too full to eat anything else. But of course, Bryn's mom cut out a nice big slice and chunked it down on the table.

"Bryn honey, come on over and taste a little bit of this."

All around us, the adults were talking and laughing and some of the uncles were arguing about who had the best car but the kids were riveted to the scene in front of them.

Somebody whispered "she's not going to eat it."

Someone else said "she has too, her mom

will make her."

Willie was very quiet, I actually got kind of worried about him because he had a weak stomach and some things just made him throw up all of a sudden if it grossed him out. Bryn's mom got a fork and took a big bite of the pie and said "man, this is good.

Here Bryn, we haven't had this pie in a long time, I want you to try a bite." Bryn closed her mouth real tight and squinched up her face and wouldn't take a bite. She refused. Then her mom got mad and said "Eat this right now, or you'll get a whipping.!"

Bryn started to cry and screamed "ok, give me a whipping, cause I ain't eating that!!" All the adults stopped talking and turned around to see what the fuss was all about. Grandma and Aunt Darcy were doing some dishes and stopped with soapy hands to see what was going on. Grandma said, "Honey, what is wrong with you. That is good pie and I made it special today. I haven't made it in a long time. I'm going to make it every year for Christmas from now on so you might as well get use to it."

Then it happened.

Bryn opened her mouth to say something and at that moment, her mom shoved in a bite of that pie and all the kids groaned at once. Bryn spit it out on the floor and Willie started to gag. His gags sounded awful. Like something was dying.

For a minute, the eyes turned from Bryn to Willie and then he started puking. All over the floor, all over his new slippers from Santa, and all over his Christmas clothes. Then another kid started puking. Before too long, the floor was awash in mashed potatoes, dumplins, turkey and ham. Uncle Jake started gagging and before you knew it, all the men were puking too.

Aunt Darcy got so mad.

She started shaking and shrieked " Stop it!!! Stop puking on Christmas!!"

Willie was crying by this time and had a complete meltdown. He screamed at the top of his lungs. "This is not Christmas! Christmas is about Jesus and Santa and presents and good food. Christmas isn't puking and making people eat toes!"

Then he turned to Uncle Jake and screamed "This is all your fault. Why did you have to bring men's feet to Christmas to put in the pie!!?"

Mom was in a state of shock. It took only moments to turn a beautiful Christmas in to a nightmare. She wanted to clean up the mess, but she was turning a little white herself. Then Willie started with the loud gagging again and by this time he was crying uncontrollably. So, she grabbed him up and took him right outside where it was nice and cold and just held him while he cried it all out.

When Grandma got over being stunned, she looked at Bryn and said "what is this all about?" "Why didn't you want to eat my pie?"

Bryn looked at Zack and then looked at me and told her what I said. At the end of the story, all eyes turned on me and I was so ashamed at what I had done to ruin Christmas. I just hung my head and could not meet anybody in the eye. Of course, Bryn forgot to tell about ruining Farmer Boy and that is what really caused the whole thing to happen.

My dad said "I never thought I would have to spank one of my kids on Christmas Day. Especially you Sis. You are the oldest."

That is when Aunt Darcy stepped in and said "Well, no reason to start today. We will just clean up this mess and she will help and that will be punishment enough."

My Dad started to say something, and my Grandma said in a really loud voice "That sounds just fine Darcy. Now, all of you get out of this kitchen while we clean up this mess."
Everybody left but me and Grandma and Aunt Darcy.

They didn't even have to ask, I just blurted the whole story out about my book and how mad I was and that the opportunity just came up and I did not think that I would end up making everybody puke on Christmas. By the time I was finished, I was crying and I thought they were both crying too, but it turned out they started laughing. Which is something I never expected.

Aunt Darcy said that this will be a Christmas to remember.

I went outside and it was starting to snow and the wind was blowing. Dad was trying to cover the new washer and dryer with a tarp until the rest of the Uncles could help him unload it. All he said to me was "don't you ever do anything like that again."

Men's Feet Pie

We made it through that Christmas, and I wanted to forget all about it. And I did, until the next Christmas time rolled around.

Grandma was going to make all the pies and desserts and wanted me to help. I was sure that we would not ever have another MinceMeat Pie for any holiday again but I was wrong. I did not really think that I should ever have anything to do with a pie like that again because of what I had done to ruin Christmas the year before. I was still ashamed every time I thought about it..

I don't know how Grandma always knew what I was thinking, but somehow she did. She said "don't you worry about it." Then I heard her on the phone talking to Aunt Darcy and laughing about something and about an hour later, Aunt Darcy showed up with a sack from the drug store. She opened it up and there were a couple of baby doll toys in it.

Grandma and Aunt Darcy started making crust dough and mixing stuff up in bowls while I sat at the counter. Then Aunt Darcy handed me a spoon and said "here, mix this up" and before I knew it I was making pies and forgetting about last Christmas. We baked those pies and when they were done and cooled down, Aunt Darcy pulled out those plastic baby dolls and started pulling off arms and legs and feet and hands. Then she and Grandma shoved all the little pieces into the pies and covered it all up with whipped cream.

Every year for Christmas after that, Grandma and Aunt Darcy would whip up those pies and I always got to help. The first time we did it, she made two pies. My dad got the first piece and acted like he was going to be mad when he pulled out a plastic foot. Aunt Darcy and Grandma both started laughing so hard and said "Aren't you the big winner today!"

So the kids all tried some of the pie and whenever somebody got a plastic body part, the whole family cheered.

We ran out of Men's Feet Pie that first Christmas we did it, so the next year, we baked an extra one. That was always the first dessert cut in to on every Christmas after that. Whenever somebody got a piece that did not have a part in it, it was kind of sad. They would actually act disappointed.

I don't know really how to explain the way I felt about those pies we made during the following years. It was like Grandma took something that I did wrong and turned it into something that we all looked forward to. It redeemed me somehow.

OUR HOUSE

    Every house on our street had kids, and for some reason, they always ended up at our place. Of course, there was a well worn dirt trail that snaked through the neighborhood between houses and along the back yards. We played together and those trails accidentally happened because of all the walking and bike riding that we did to get to each other. The street was a straight road, and there was a sidewalk that ran along the whole street, but there were better ways to go and get together with the friends.

    For example, one of the houses had this tree that we all liked. I don't know what the name of it was, but in the spring and summer it had these whispy pink flowers that looked like they came from Hawaii or some exotic island. Right there in the middle of the street, in the middle of New

Madrid was a place that we all gathered at and pretended like we were on a deserted island just like Gilligan. There were other exciting parts of the trail too. Behind one house, there was some sort of drainage ditch but we found some pieces of wood and made a bridge. The boys all thought that they were Evel Knieval though and liked to jump that ditch on their bikes. They would start off on their bikes two backyards away and get to going really fast and then, with handle bars streaming, they would make the big jump.

If the daredevils crashed we all groaned and shook our heads but helped them to get untangled from the ditch. But whenever somebody made it, the cheers and screams could be heard all over the neighborhood. Everybody's house had something. It could be a tree, or a jump, of a place where we had built a fort to hang out in on the hot days. Some of the kids were famous in the neighborhood because they always had a fridge full of popsicles. We had the only basketball goal and my dad had painted lines on the driveway so that it looked just like a real ball court.

Every day there would be jumbles and lines of kid's bikes in the yard while we played basketball, or just hung out until it was time for everyone to go home. There was always something going on outside.

Inside, our house looked like most of the other houses on the street but I always thought ours was a little messier. For one thing, we had the big aquariums sitting right next to the piano in the living room. And there was always something piled

Men's Feet Pie

on top of the piano. You could see through the living room right in to the kitchen.

The phone was hung on the wall in the kitchen. It was a lime green, with a twisted cord that stretched all the way across the kitchen to the table. This was a point where there was a dividing wall between the kitchen and the living room. On that wall was the best evidence we had of a family tree.

One day, dad needed to write down a phone number, and didn't have a piece of paper. So, he picked up a permanent marker and wrote down Aunt Bert's phone number right on the wall. Now, this was not a whole wall, it was rather the 4 inch space where two walls meet. Over time, that 4 inch section of wall developed a character and became command central of the household.

Mom hated it. From the simple beginnings of that one phone number, it became the most complete listing of all of our family members. Dad wrote down all of his sibling's phone numbers, and then the school numbers. Dad also hated trying to find the phone book in the junk drawer so he drilled a hole in the phone book and hammered this big nail in to the wall and hung the phone book on it.

Bobbie Sue was only about three feet tall and wrote in marker the phone number of her friends on the bottom. The numbers were always written in markers, but not always the same color of markers. When Willie was about four, he learned to put a big soup pot upside down on the floor, climb up and then pull himself up on the washing machine. Then he could reach the phone and he called every long distance phone number on the wall.

We all ate in the kitchen together every night at the big white table that was Grandma's gift to mom and dad when they got the house. It was a used table and had already seen plenty of family dinners.

The routine for dinner was almost always the same. Koolaid made for us kids (by me, because I was the oldest) and tea for mom and dad. Sometimes, I made the dinner but it was usually when we had sandwiches or something simple like fried hot dogs and macaroni and cheese. Which, by the way, was one of our favorite meals.

At least once a week, we had breakfast for supper but we never made biscuits to go with the gravy, we just tore up Wonder bread and piled up the gravy on top. That was one of Willies favorite days. During the summer, he would get to go out to the garden and pick the tomatoes that we sliced up to go with the scrambled eggs. We weren't too fancy during the week. There were a couple of times that Mom tried to fancy us up though.

ROCKS, STICKS AND GRASS

When Mom went through her phase of fancy cooking, she tried to introduce us to all sorts of flavors and make us appreciate the fine art of dining. Now, I've already explained how important food was in the family and how everything revolved around it. So, it was kind of a shock when Mom decided that the food we ate every day just wasn't good enough.

It all started with a tv show that she watched with a woman named Julia, who talked funny and put all sorts of stuff in her food. Now, in our family, we had our favorites. Tried and trusted, bonafide favorites. During the summer, the top pick was sour cream and cucumbers. Usually the cucumbers were picked right out of the garden. The ingredients were simple, sour cream, peeled sliced cucumbers, salt and pepper and nothing else.

One day, we came in for supper and mom had this strange look in her eyes. She said that supper would be on in a few minutes and she wanted us to wash our hands and comb our hair. Well, that should have tipped us off that something was wrong, because we always washed our hands, but we never had to comb our hair. But, we did it and when we came to the table mom brought out the big green tupperware bowl that she always made the sour cream and cukes in. We settled in at the table and started to pass around the bowls and Mom took off the lid of the cukes. She plopped a big spoon full on my plate and started smiling at me.

I looked down while she was giving everybody else some and it didn't look right. There were thousands of tiny pieces of grass in my cukes. When Bobbie Sue got hers, she started crying that something had got in to our food. "Now hush......"mom said. I made these a special way with an herb called dill. You are supposed to use dill with cucumbers and I thought we would all try it.

"I don't wanna try it" wailed Willie,

Dad even said "now mom, why would you go and mess up some perfectly good cucumbers?"

Mom started shrieking in her high pitched way and said "none of you have even tried it yet and after all of the trouble I went through to make it special at least you can put a bite in to your mouths and taste it." She glared at dad and he said "ok mom, we are all going to take a bite." He slowly looked at each one of us and nodded. "We will all take a bite together ."

So, ever so slowly, we each put a bit of Sour Cream and Cucumbers with Grass in it on our forks and lifted it to our mouths. We weren't looking at the food, but at each other to gage reactions. At once, we all put our forks in our mouths and closed our lips with eyes closed . Then, in a convulsive explosion, all mouths were emptied right back on to the plates with the awful stuff.

Willie started to wail again and dad looked at mom with a murderous rage and said "don't you ever do that again." He got up and threw the bowl of Sour Cream and Cukes with Grass out the back door.

That was just the first of many things that she tried. I will admit, some of the things she made we really liked, like the time she wrapped bacon around shrimp and cooked it in the oven. Even dad was smiling when he ate those. But, of course, mom only did that once or twice then decided that shrimp was just too expensive to feed to kids. We also liked stuffed peppers and they became a staple at the house. All dripping with tomato sauce.

Some of the things she made tasted good, but had funny little twigs in them like the time she made rosemary chicken. She also used peppercorns in the sauce and they looked like little rocks floating around and tasted too strong. The stuff was all tied up in a little cloth bag and was supposed to stay that way and be taken out right before we ate, but the bag broke open and mom thought it looked pretty so she left it all in the pan. My dad liked the taste of the chicken but threw such a fit when he got a bit of the twigs stuck between his teeth that he made mom promise to never cook with it again. So, he fished out all the twigs and then got a big bite of the peppercorn rocks and threw his fork down in total disgust at the ruining of a perfectly good chicken.

She made one more attempt to fancy up the sour cream and cukes. This time she tried an herb called parsley. We had company coming over for supper and a glut of cucumbers, so of course it was on the menu. I was in the kitchen when she was making it. I glanced over and could not believe my eyes when I saw her sprinkle something green into the bowl. She looked over at me and noticed my concerns and said, "Don't worry. This is called parsley and the herb doesn't add any flavor, it only makes it look pretty. See, she held out a spoon for me to try. I tasted it and it did not taste funny. But I said, "That's not too bad mom, but just to be on the safe side maybe we should make some the good way in case dad tries to throw this bowl. Then we will at least have some."

After that, she never did try to fancy up the sour cream and cukes. It was always one of our favorite things to have in the summer. The best part was after all of the cucumbers were eaten, there was this great juice left in the bottom of the bowl. We would actually fight over who got to drink the leftover juice, or if there wasn't enough, we would scrape it out with a spoon and slurp it like it was ice cream.

Changing

    The Gas gauge is less than half full and my dad would throw a fit if he knew I let it get this low, so I need to stop going down memory lane and find a gas station. I'm still in Kansas and the snow just started up again. The towns are so far apart that I'm afraid I will run out of gas before I get to one. I pulled over to the side of the road and got my map out to see how far I would have to go. Looks like about 30 miles there is a small town and surely there will be a gas station there.
    When I got out of the car to fill up, the cold hit me like a wave and froze my nose hairs. I have never felt cold like a Kansas cold. The wind howls across that flat land and you feel like it could pick you up and take you flying across the prairie. I don't know how the Ingalls family traveled in a covered wagon across this land during the winter. They must have been some tough people. With my teeth chattering, I filled the tank, checked the tires

to make sure they weren't flat and scraped snow and ice chunks off the back window. Then I went to the bathroom and used the pay phone to call my dad again and got back on the road.

I felt kind of exhilarated. Cold does that to me sometimes, like it makes everything cleaner and sharper. As soon as I got back into the car and started it up, I stopped thinking about when I was young growing up and started thinking about high school. Life started changing a lot for me during the summer before I started high school. And of course, it involves books.

Grandpa had stopped over at the house one day and said that I needed to go to see Grandma, because she had something for me. So, I got on my bike and rode over to see what the surprise was.

As soon as I walked in, I knew something good was going to happen, because Grandma was smiling really big. "Hey Sis, go look on the kitchen table.

Grandma and Aunt Darcy had gone to a garage sale early that morning. They came home with a bunch of big paper IGA sacks full of stuff. I looked in the first one and it was full of turnips.

"Grandma, are we gonna cook turnips for supper?" I asked.

" No child, look in the other one."

While I was looking, Grandma was popping popcorn. I had movie theater popcorn once, Grandma's was much better. Because Grandma popped her corn in bacon grease. It always smelled so good. Grandma kept a big metal can right beside the stove. She made bacon and eggs every morning and after the bacon was fried in the cast iron skillet, she would pour the grease in this can. Then, when she wanted to season something, she would just grab a big spoon and get out a dollop of grease plunk it down on the pan. She didn't like to use lard unless she was frying chicken. That particular skillet was not used for anything but frying bacon. After she poured the grease off, she would just wipe the skillet out with a paper towel and consider it clean and ready for tomorrow's bacon. The can never got full because every time grandma cooked something she would season it with bacon grease.

As the first kernal of corn popped, releasing all of its good popcorn smell, I looked in to the other bag. It was full of books. Tons of them. I accidentally ripped the bag trying to get them out. They all tumbled out of the bag and spilled out all over the table. They were all romance novels and I felt my face getting red like it does when I am embarrassed. All of the covers had pictures of half naked men with big muscles and long hair picking up frail women with one hand. Some just had the faces of men who looked like Greek gods.

"Um...Grandma, can I read this stuff?"

" Sure you can, just don't tell your mom."

"And if you get to any words you don't understand, just skip over it and go on. There might be some racy stuff in there, but the books were free and we are not gonna waste a book by not reading it, even if it is kind of sleazy."

"So pick one out," she said as she poured two sticks of melted butter over our bacon grease popcorn. "I have the tea ready and we'll just go in to the living room and read."

So, off we went, and grandma pulled us out two quilts, the ones with the red yarn sticking up out of the squares, and she settled on the big couch and I got the little couch. She got her book and I got mine, and we read and ate popcorn and drank sweet tea until we both fell asleep. That is how I learned about the ways of the world.

I considered myself far more educated than my friends and I imagined that Sister Bridget would break rulers over my head if she knew the words I was learning. About passionate steamy kisses…and that men could sometimes have quivering torsos and throbbing members…whatever that meant.

So, after that, Grandma started going to garage sales just to buy us books. We never knew what she would come home with. Sometimes they were grown up novels, and sometimes they were books on how to do something, like how to shear sheep. Even though we did not have any sheep, we read the book. Like Grandma said, we were not gonna waste a book by not reading it if it was right there in front of us. So, Sundays were book days.

My life really changed that summer that I turned 13. There were a lot of things that were new, like going to high school and getting to pick out the clothes I wore instead of wearing a uniform. But the biggest change was in the types of books I read. I went from Trixie Belden and Pippi Longstocking straight to Harlequin Romance Novels. And my world was forever changed.

After the big lunch that we always had at Grandma's house, everybody in the family just left us alone. If they wanted to do something, grandma would tell them that we were busy and to go in the kitchen or the back room and watch tv.

One day, Grandma and dad got in to this big fight because he came over on a Sunday and told me to get my head outta the books and go out and do something. He said that it was not natural that a kid did not have any friends and would sit with her nose stuck in a book for hours. Besides, it would make my eyes go bad.

Grandma pinched her mouth together and said "you listen here......that kid is the only kid in this family that likes to read. She is going to be the first one to go to college....you hear me. If she wants to sit in here and read for ten hours a day she is going to at my house. She has to know big words and she ain't going to learn them at that catholic school where they make them recite verses all day long. If her eyes go bad, I'll buy her some glasses."

Dad didn't know what to say, 'cause grandma never pinched her lips together unless she was really mad. So he just turned around and walked out. He never said another word about my books after that. In fact, he built me some book cases to keep in my room and before long, they were covered up with stacks of books.

There has only been one book that I wish I had never read. It came from one of those garage sales. It was called Helter Skelter and told the story of an evil man named Charlie Manson. I was about 15 when I read that book and I had nightmares so bad that I actually got in bed with my mom and dad, which really freaked them out. My dad threw that book in the trash and told me I couldn't finish it. I was glad. But I made sure to not tell Grandma that we threw away a book

The Garden and Grandpa

The summer before going to high school was one of my favorite times. Partially because of the books I was getting to read now but something else happened that summer that I will remember my whole life. It was the summer that I learned about Grandpa.

Grandma and Aunt Darcy had decided that they were going to make the garden at Aunt Darcy's really big and actually have a real planting area with everything lined up in rows. This was not Aunt Darcy's way, but Grandma told her that the grandkids would help with all the weeding. So, one Saturday early in the Spring, Grandpa borrowed a tractor for the day to go and till up the soil, and get it ready for planting.

We pulled up into the yard to find Aunt Darcy sitting on the front porch with her guitar singing to her cats. The windows were down in the car and we could hear her before we even got out of the car.

She was in the mood for Janis Joplin and was crooning Bobby McGee. I liked the way she sang. She tried to sing in a pretty voice but with her Southeast Missouri twang, she sounded like a country singer. She would really get into the songs she sang and make all sorts of faces and really act out the words. The cats loved it.

All of us kids tumbled out of the car and looked over at Grandma and Grandpa who were both smiling. Grandma put her finger to her lips and motioned for us to be quiet until the song was over. Aunt Darcy hated it if we interrupted her songs before they were over because she couldn't get back into the groove.

When the song was over, the cats were all humming. Aunt Darcy took a big swig of her bottle of Tab and lit a cigarette and looked up and said "did y'all know that if you talk to your plants and sing to them they grow better and produce more vegetables?"

Grandpa shook his head and looked at the ground but said, "that's a fine idea Darcy. You and the cats can sing to the garden all you want, but I'm not going to be singing to the tractor."
With that being said, Grandpa went to till up the big patch of ground and me and Grandma and Willie and Zack and Bryn piled up on to the porch to show Aunt Darcy all of the seeds we got to go pick out.

Willie had picked out nothing but flowers. Grandma said that was just fine, he could plant all the flowers along the edge of the garden. Bryn was making fun of him being a boy and wanting to grow pretty flowers and Aunt Darcy said "you just wait a

Men's Feet Pie

cotton pickin minute! Gardens are supposed to have flowers for the bees and to make the tomatoes happy." That shut Bryn up pretty quick, and Willie just grinned.

Grandpa had the tractor going all morning and the rest of us sat on the porch getting the seeds started in little pots so they would have a head start growing before we put them in to the ground. Aunt Darcy was right in the middle of teaching the little kids some songs to sing to the seeds when Grandpa walked up to the porch all sweaty and dirty and plopped down in the chair. He said "that is a fine tractor, I wonder what my dad would have done if he would have had something like that when we were growing up and he was trying to feed 11 kids."

Willie looked up and said "why, couldn't you just go to the grocery store?" Grandpa just smiled over at Grandma and said "Well, things were a little different back then."

Willie said "How different?"

That one question seemed to take Grandpa by surprise, and he said "it just was different, that's all." For one thing, we didn't just go to the store every time we needed something. I had 10 brothers and sisters and we grew almost everything we ate. My mom made all of our clothes and since I was in the middle, I got the hand-me-downs. We had chickens and every year we butchered a hog if we were lucky enough to have one that year. It took every one of us kids to help grow and make the things that we needed."

Willie said "That's cool, I wanna butcher a hog." Grandma snorted and said "you would not like it at all!" "When I was a kid we did the same thing. We grew up so poor but did not know it because everybody else was poor too. Getting ahold of a nickel was as hard as getting ahold of a five dollar bill."

Then Willie asked "Why?"

Grandpa took a sip of sweet tea and got a faraway look in his eyes. Even though he didn't talk much, we knew he was about to say something when he cleared his throat. He told us a story.

Grandpa and Grandma grew up during a time called the Great Depression. He was little, but he still remembered everything about that time. The family had a farm and struggled to grow anything at all because it was so dry and hot. The work never stopped no matter what season it was. Most of the kids didn't have shoes to wear so they ran around barefooted all summer, and in the winter they took turns wearing shoes. But then something happened to change his life.

Grandpa started by saying "I wasn't much older than Sis when I got sent from the only place I had ever known all the way to Montana."

When he was 17, he got signed up for something called the CCC. The Civilian Conservation Corp. It was 1938 and the Depression had been going on for as long as he remembered. The CCC sent him from Southeast Missouri to a place in Montana called Glacier National Park.

He boarded a train and it took about 4 days to get there. After coming from the struggles that his family had, he felt like he was living like a king. There was a bunch of boys all his age and they were in need of a job and sent to Montana to build roads and buildings and trails.

When he first got there, he was issued new clothes, which was the first time that he had new clothes in his whole life. They did exercises every morning and had three meals a day. When he sat down to have his first meal. He felt so bad.

He said " I was feeling sorry for myself because I was so far away from my family and wanted to go home. Then I looked down at the table and had a real plate made out of China with a roll and a pat of butter on it. Then I felt bad about feeling sorry for myself, because there I was, eating off a plate with butter while my brothers and sisters were happy to have lard out of a tin bucket to put on their biscuits."

Willie asked him if it was cold there. Grandpa said "yes, it seemed like it was always winter, but summer time was beautiful. While he was remembering Montana, he told us that it seemed like a different world. "You can't imagine those big ole mountains, and how blue the water was in the lakes."

In the mornings when they boys would get up, they would have to walk by the garbage dump area and it would be covered with black bears scrambling all over it eating the scraps. He got paid twenty five dollars a month for working for Roosevelt's Tree Army, which was what they called it. Eighteen dollars of that money was sent home to his family. It made their lives better because now they could buy flour and fabric to make clothes.

Willie asked him if they still had the CCC because he wanted to go to Montana and see those bears for himself. Grandpa shook his head and said "No, those days are over. The government started the CCC as a work relief program to give people jobs. People were starving all over the country and the government had to do something. Young men were sent to camps in different states to help plant trees, build trails and roads, or to do any kind of work that was needed. "President Roosevelt was a smart man" said Grandpa, this country was in big trouble and we had to have some kind of work to do."

Zack said "well, I would have just fished for my supper!" Grandpa said there was very little fish to be had. People fished out the ponds and the river was so full of mud that you couldn't hardly catch a thing. Besides, everybody had that idea and a lot of people went hungry. And, you need more than just a fish to live on. The men needed to work to provide for their family. And there was no work to be found anywhere."

"So," said Grandpa, "The CCC was a New Deal Program to put young men to work and to keep the conservation of the National Parks." We didn't know it at the time, but that was the best training we had for what was to come next. We operated like the military, with calisthenics every morning, three meals a day, job duties, and we had to keep our bunks made. Most of the boys that showed up for these camps were practically starved, but they got regular food and put on some weight."

"I was in the CCC for two years and then

went back home to Missouri. I had no idea that I would be leaving home again but this time I was going a lot further than Montana."

Then Grandpa stood up and said it was time for us to go home.

I said "Grandpa, what came next?"

Willie grabbed his hand and asked him "Where did you go?"

Grandpa shook his head and said "That is another story for another time. We will come back next Saturday and if you still want to hear about it, I will tell you what happened next."

The next Saturday, we all went back to Aunt Darcy's but this time my sister came with us. She heard about the bear story from Willie and Zack and wanted to know what the next part was going to be. We worked all morning plucking out weeds and picking up rocks from the newly plowed garden and throwing them over the fence. Then it was time to stop. Grandma and Aunt Darcy had made sandwiches and tea for lunch and we all found a spot on the porch with the cats and waited for Grandpa to tell us about where he went next.

He took a sip of his tea and cleared his throat. "I told you all last week that I got to go back to Missouri after leaving the CCC in Montana and all of the bears. There were still hard times but there was even harder times a coming. In December, 1941, our country was attacked by the Japanese. This meant war. So, on July 10, 1942, I caught a bus from New Madrid to go to Jefferson City to begin my training with the Army. I was to be a medic."

"I trained in a lot of places in the States before I was shipped out. I trained in Arkansas and Texas. I went to the desert training camp at the Mojave Desert. Now I have already told you that I was to be a medic for the Army. When they gave us our training, they decided if you were going to be a surgical technician or a medical technician. They took me in to assist on an operation and I saw blood and got sick. Then they said I would have to be a medical technician because I could not stand blood."

"Then, after all of this training, we went to San Francisco, and loaded a small Liberty Ship. The night before, we were up all night loading barrels. When we got on to that ship, the Captain came aboard with a radio in his hands and called for two small tugs to pull us out to sea for a mile and a half before he started the motor. And when that motor started, the Captain of the ship says "we're on our way." He didn't say where we were on our way to, but anyway, the first three days we were out to sea you get to feeling awful bad."

Willie asked "what made you feel bad?"

Grandpa told him "It was that water, moving and tossing you around. But, you kinda get over that, and when the water gets rough or it starts to storm, you get sick again."

"When we were 15 days out, they gave us a talk down in the mess hall to tell us where we were going. They said we were going to New Guinea. He says everybody get you a knife. If a big snake gets on you there's no way you can get them off except cut them off."

"Well, I walked out the hatch and there sits an old Italian. He was sitting there just whittling away. He had a cigar box full of knives. I wondered why he had a cigar box full of knives. But I said to him "what would you take for one of them knives?" He says five dollars. Well, I thought if one of them snakes gets around me five dollars ain't gonna do me no good, so I gave him five dollars for the knife."

Zack asked him if it was a big knife.

"Not so big, but I reckon I could have killed a snake with it if I had to."

So, we went on to Milne Bay. We went to the first place in New Guinea where we stayed one night. Then we went up the shore to Finch Haven, Anyway, we made about three stops up the coast of New Guinea. All the time I was there, nobody ever saw a snake because the natives used them as a food.

Bobbie Sue said "Gross, eating snakes! Why did they eat snakes?"

Grandpa told her "there's no civilization on parts of New Guinea. They ate what they could. The natives ate anything they could get…like a wild animal. Anything they could find, they would put it all in a pot and cook it together. New Guinea is a big island there were parts that had civilization and parts where there was no civilization. We were on the part with no civilization. In New Guinea a pig was their main food."

"I wouldn't have believed it if I had not seen it for myself, but I saw women walking down the road…with no shirt on… carrying a piglet in one arm and nurse it on her breast. She would use the other breast to nurse the baby. The woman would carry all of her belongings in a big pot that she carried on her head. The men were big and strong but they would walk behind the woman and if she laid down or got tired, he would beat her with a stick. The men would trade the pig for another woman. There was no civilization."

All of us groaned at once. "Really, they would let a pig nurse from the woman?"

"They sure did" said Grandpa. "It was common to see. As poor as they were, pigs were valuable and those women would fatten up a pig with her own breast milk."

Grandpa cleared his throat again and said "now there was some awful sad things that happened while we were on New Guinea. We never did see any Japanese while we were on New Guinea, but we had another killer. It was the fever."

"The jungle fever was a killer. There was dengue fever, there was malaria. There was typhoid, there was typhus. Typhus was a killer. Typhus was caused by a small mite. You couldn't see them with your naked eye. But whenever they bit a person, they leave a little round red ring. In the middle of that ring would be pus. Some patients would have three bites on them. Don't know whether they was all done by one mite, or whether they was three different mites. But whenever you get bit by one of them mites, your chances of living was 50/50."

"Since I was a medic, I was the one giving

Men's Feet Pie

the treatment. The treatment for the typhus was penicillin, give 40,000 units of penicillin…..that was the beginning shot. Then they got 20,000 units for 15 days thereafter. They got sulfa drugs, they got codeine, they got barbital. Then at the end of 15 days was the crisis period. They knew whether they would get well. They would never get well, but they would get over it. Get better or die. They either turned better or worse after those 15 days."

"If they turned worse they put them in a separate tent. The boys knew they were gonna die. It was pitiful. One morning, seven boys died in that tent between the hours of 8 and 10. It was pitiful….such a sad thing. Now one time, one of the places I was in, 50 percent of 'em was down with the jungle fever. Now, I might give a little add on here. When somebody came up missing in New Guinea, it was chances are that the jungle fever got them."

Zack held his hand up to ask a question. "Grandpa why didn't they just put on bug spray?"

"Oh, they sprayed around our tent for the mites. Now those mites were carried on rats and mice….They come out of the laguna grass. They would run out of the laguna grass and run across your bedding, or you could walk through that grass and get em on you that way. Most of the time when you would lay down on your bedding that's when they would bite you. But that one tent….where they took the boys after the 15 days….7 boys died in that tent in one morning…they all died between the hours of 8 to 10."

Grandpa had to stop talking for a minute and

take a big drink of his tea. I could see that his hand was shaking. It seemed like just for a minute, he was back in that tent where those boys died. After he put his tea glass down, he stood up and stretched his back and said "Well, the rocks are chucked out of the garden and I am finished telling stories for the day."

Willie wanted to know "Grandpa, is that the whole story?"

Grandpa shook his head and said, "no, there's more. If you still want to hear about it, next week I will meet you here on this front porch after we get those plants into the ground."

So, all during that week, all any of us talked about was that story and about the pigs and the fever and Grandpa being in that tent trying to take care of all those boys. Some of the other cousins heard about what was going on at Aunt Darcy's on Saturday and decided that they wanted to help with the gardening.

The Pink Pontiac was already full of grandkids so a couple of the other aunts had to bring their kids over. They brought some picnic baskets full of potted meat and crackers, Vienna sausages, pimento cheese and other things to set out for lunch.

When we showed up, Aunt Darcy had a cooler full of Tab and some Grape soda for us kids and a big pot of sweet tea for Grandpa and the other adults. Willie had wanted to ask Grandpa some questions during the week about the pigs and Bobbie Sue wanted to know what kind of stuff the women carried in the pots on their head, but Grandma told them that Grandpa had never told anyone these stories, not even her, and he would only talk about it on Saturday. So that rule was made that the only time we could ask about those stories was on Saturday when Grandpa was in the mood to talk about it.

Saturday morning rolled around and Willie didn't even seem upset about missing his cartoons anymore. He was ready to go before anyone else and sat on the front steps of our house waiting for Grandma and Grandpa to come pick us up. I know how early he was up because I was up and so was my sister. We were all anxious to go.

We got to Aunt Darcy's at about the same time as some of the cousins and their moms and it looked like there was a family dinner going on, with all of the cars lining the gravel road.

All morning, we planted the little seedlings, and plucked out any weeds in the garden that had popped up and tried to keep the rows straight. Then it was time for lunch.

Everybody ate and took up their spots on the porch. The cats even knew it was time for the story. They seemed to settle in and pay attention too.

Grandpa took a sip of tea, and said "Now where was I?"

Zack said "you were on New Guinea watching those women nurse a pig on one tit and a baby on the other!" Everybody laughed and Grandpa said, "yes, I saw some crazy things on New Guinea. Those natives could do things that didn't seem human. One time, I was looking up at a coconut tree, and there were a group of about 5 natives. I pointed to the coconut up top, and quick as a flash, one of those men climbed up that tree like he was flying up it. He got me a coconut and I gave him a cigarette for it. He took off back to his village to show off the cigarette.

"Now that same group of men saw me on the beach one afternoon. Whenever I would get off work, I would go down to the beach and the tide would be out. I would pick up seashells. Got 4 or 5 shells a day so that I could make bracelets and necklaces to send back home. This group of men saw what I was looking for. They went over to a big rock and lifted it up and pulled out about a gallon full of shells. I took those shells back to my tent and buried them under my bunk. The ants went to work on them and cleaned them up really good. Then I drilled some holes in them and made necklaces to send back home."

Bryn asked "where are those necklaces and bracelets now?" Grandma piped up and said "I have those put away."

Grandpa took up his story. "Now when we went up the coast of New Guinea, a lot of times we bivuouaced. Just right out in the open. You dug a hole and you stayed in that hole all night long…you couldn't get out of that hole or the guard would shoot you. We stayed there about nine months. There was one more thing that was bad there. That was the jungle rot. I've got a place of that jungle rot on my finger now. There was no cure for that."

The little kids all got up and crowded around Grandpa so that they could see the scars of jungle rot on his hand. He let them all touch that place. Then he held it up for us to see. He said "I got jungle rot and I also got something called malaria. I was awful sick."

"It was so hot there. It seemed like you would never get cool again. That place was a breeding ground for fevers and jungle rot and if somebody got wounded, the heat would stop them from getting better. If they got a fever, there was no way we could cool them down. We did not have any ice, so all we had was medicine."

I raised my hand to ask Grandpa a question. "Grandpa, I thought we were fighting the Germans in World War 2. Why did they send you all the way to that island?"

Grandpa said, "it wasn't only the Germans we were fighting. The Japanese had bombed us at Pearl Harbor, remember. They also invaded some islands in the Pacific and that was why we got sent to New Guinea. The Japs were there and we went to kick them out."

"Couldn't they fight them off themselves?"

"No, they were so poor that there was no way they could have fought off the Japanese without our help. They cut the poor native people all to pieces. They were as helpless as a little kid. They cut them all to pieces and took everything they had. When any of the natives would do some work for us or help us, the Army paid them with costume jewelry and they would give them color for their hair. They wanted their hair to be red…I think it was peroxide….they liked to be dressed up.

"When we left New Guinea, we went to Marti. And that was the first place that we came into contact with the Japanese."

"Umm Grandpa, was there a whole bunch of soldiers with you to shoot the Japanese?"

"No, we did not travel with a bunch of soldiers. I was in a small group of the Army. We were a Special Unit that was not attached to any Division. The whole company was about one hundred men. We had 13 doctors, 2 dentists and a part time chaplain. The rest of the Unit was made of medics and support. This little outfit could pack up and move in an hour if we had to."

To get to Marti, we traveled on a LSD, which is a Dock Landing Ship. It was a small vessel that could take us right up to shore. When we got to Marti, the Japanese came in and dropped a bomb on the bow of the LSD. When that bomb was dropped, the Captain went plumb wild. It scared him to death."

"We were loaded with gas and oil and all of our equipment. All of our equipment went with us. They kicked us off of that boat so fast. The commanding officer was a surgeon. They had him rolling barrels of oil just like they did the privates. That was terrifying, to be pulling in and get bombed right away."

"We set up on Marti and Tokyo Rose was on the air all the time. She said you people on Marti are gonna get blasted off of there tonight! Sure enough, that night the airplanes came and hit that oil depot all night long." You could see the big 55 gallon drums go sky high and burst into flames."

"Grandpa, how did Tokyo Rose know that was going to happen? Was she on our side and warning us?"

"Oh No! She was not on our side. She would come on the radio speaking in English and talk and say bad things. She tried to get us all scared and feeling bad so that we would give up. But she would talk as though she was friendly but at the same time tell us we were all going to get bombed. You hear her on the radio and get to feeling bad."

"And it wasn't just her on the radio. You could turn the radio off. We had Washing Machine Charlie bothering us all the time."

Zack laughed and said "Washing Machine Charlie? He doesn't sound so scary. What did he do?"

Grandpa just looked at Zack. "Washing Machine Charlie was awful. It would be a Japanese plane flying right over where we were. They called him Washing Machine Charlie because the sound his plane made sounded like a loud washing machine, not like a regular plane. Sometimes he would just fly over and drop flares, or just keep flying over to wake us all up so that we could not sleep at night. Whenever you heard that sound you knew that you were not going to get any sleep the rest of the night. You would stay awake and then the next day not be able to think because you were so tired. Sometimes, he would come around and drop bombs on the unit. One time, he dropped one bomb and it was about 10 feet away from where our bunks were."

" But here's something you might want to know about the conventional bombs. If you will get in your hole, they almost have to hit direct on you in order to hurt you. One time a bomb hit, and a Seargent got shrapnel in his leg because he didn't get in his hole."

"It was bad alright. Bad to be away from home and getting malaria and jungle rot and seeing boys die. Tokyo Rose and Washing Machine Charlie could make every day a misery and you get to feeling really low."

" Another thing about Marti. General MacArthur came there. He came several times. He would come in with a little twin engine seaplane. When he got close to the beach he would the door and get out his walking cane and feel how deep the water is. Then he crawls out of that seaplane and walks to the shore. Back in the states, the newspapers would all say "MacArthur wades ashore again" and show a picture of him. I went to see him one time."

Grandpa stood up to leave. We all stared at him to see if he was going to tell us more of the story or if we would have to wait till next Saturday. With a final drink of his sweet tea, he said "I guess I will be here again next week if any of you want to hear more."

Then he turned and walked straight to the Pink Pontiac and left Grandma to gather us all up. I was a little shocked, because that wasn't his way, you know, to leave Grandma to carry everything to the car. But she seemed to think that it was just fine and as she watched him walk to the car, she started gathering everything up and taking her time about it. I think she thought that he must need a little time to himself.

Men's Feet Pie

Next Saturday rolled around and the whole family showed back up again. Aunt Darcy just could not believe all the help she had in the garden. We had the garden watered and weeded and it was time to stake the tomatoes. So she brought out all her old pantyhose that she kept stored in the eggs they came in.

She was so funny about that. She would not buy pantyhose unless they were the L'Eggs kind because the others were no good for staking tomatoes. Anyway, that is what she said. I think she only bought those because she liked the plastic eggs they came in. So, she came out to the garden with a basket of those pantyhose in the eggs clacking around and said "while you all are getting the tomatoes staked, we are going to grill some hot dogs and hamburgers for story time." That got us moving pretty quick.

So, hot and sweaty, we all plopped down on the front porch with our burgers and chips and waited for the story to start.

Grandpa took up his spot and began. I told you that we were on Marti "If I wasn't working, I would prowl. I would prowl down to the beach. I would go swimming. There was big coral rock. And they are sharp as a razor blade. When I went to get out, a big wave hit me. And threw me up against that sharp coral and it took them a half a day to patch me up from the cuts from that coral. We stayed there about three months. There was 158 air raids. Air raid doesn't mean that you are getting bombed, it means that enemy aircraft are in the area. They could be a pretty good way off when the sirens would go off. While we were there, the Japanese made a landing on the island."

"When we left there, we loaded up and went to sea. And we stayed at sea for 16 days. All this time that I was on a boat, 5 months and 22 days, I slept in a hammock stretched between vehicles. When we woke up one morning, we were sitting in the middle of a convoy, as far as the eye could see. Big battleships, circling that convoy just like a hen rounding up her chickens. Well, when we got close to the Phillipines, the Japanese struck the convoy. There were probably 850,000 to a million men in that convoy. All floating at once. They all worked and operated as one. Can you believe that. With precision. They attacked and America planes were trying to protect the convoy. But it came over the intercom to let the Japanese planes into the convoy. So the American planes pulled away to let the Japanese planes come in."

"But the thing was, at the rear, at the stern of each boat is a smoke pot. They turned them smoke pots on and it turned daylight into dark. And the Japanese bombers couldn't see where they were going. But they still came in. They missed. They did get one LSD but it only took a little damage. Some of the men got shrapnel, but they took care of their own wounded and sick. Two tugs came along and took that LSD out of the convoy and they threw the scrap plane overboard and then brought the LSD back to the convoy right where it was. There was never a demonstration like there was with this fighting. The sky lit up. You could the bullets hitting the planes. Every twelfth shot was a tracer.

Men's Feet Pie

But they just kept coming. The Japanese destroyed their own planes when they came into the convoy."

"Then we went on to the Phillipines. There is where the big battle was...in the Phillipines. We had to go over the board from the LSD to the LCI which is a landing ship. They throw a big rope ladder, which would go over half the LSD over the side. There would be a lot of guys on there at once, and it pulls away from the boat and it's hard to go down. But you throw your equipment and everything down and someone will grab it for you. We had to go ashore and go across the whole island to Clark field. The Filipinos had scattered the Japanese out and had killed worlds of 'em. The ditches were filled with dead Japanese."

"We set up in an old building. I had a ward at the top of that old building and you could hear the shells. The shells are scary. The bombs don't bother you, but the shells will scare you. One time, I was on the second floor carrying the guys up something to eat. When those shells started falling, down those stairs they came. Those shells were absolutely scary. But things were really happening.

Corrigedor, was a small island. That is where the Japanese took most of the prisoners. And Bataan.... Corregidor is like a big hill out in the ocean. I was talking to the prisoners the night they came in and we took care of them. They said that the Japanese came in there wave after wave after wave. There was no way that anybody could ever escape. They took those prisoners and the put them in prison camps, starved them to death and the women they treated them like they were dogs. We didn't stay there long until the prisoners from Bataan and Corrigedor started coming in."

When the war first started, there were 2200 men that were taken prisoner. There were only 400 left out of that bunch that was still alive. They were so pitiful."

Grandpa had to stop talking for a minute and take a drink of tea. He would not look up at any of us. He just stared at the porch for a minute. It was so quiet and nobody moved, Then, while he was choking back sobs, he looked up and yelled to the sky.

"Nothing but bones! It was terrible. We had to take care of them boys. I don't know how they endured what they did to stay alive. They were so emaciated that they did not even look human. We did the best we could with them and then we put them on a hospital ship and shipped them out. That was horror, what horror really was." Grandpa was still sobbing and trying to get the words out. All he managed to say was " That is what war is. It is horror. They were starved and looked like skeletons."

Everybody on the porch was crying by this time. We had never seen our Grandpa like this and he had never told anybody that he was there. We had no idea that a place could be so bad to make Grandpa this upset so many years later.

One by one, each of us got up and walked over to him. There were 12 of us kids on that porch surrounding him while he sat on that metal chair and cried. We all just kind of fell on him and held on while his sobs shook the whole porch. Grandma and Aunt Darcy and all of the other aunts were crying too but stayed back while we helped Grandpa cry.

That day ended and we were all so polite and quiet to each other while we packed everything up. Grandma asked Aunt Darcy to drive some kids home and she took Grandpa home just by herself.

The next Saturday rolled around and we all showed up again. Grandma said that Grandpa was going to finish telling his stories, and we all were a little nervous about what was coming next. The garden was in full bloom and starting to have vegetables show up so we all weeded and cleaned up the area and exclaimed over how quick everything was growing. Then it was time. So, all of us took up our place on the porch to hear what happened next.

Grandpa started out just like he always did and did not say one word about what happened the week before. "They moved us down to a Phillipine prison. Units came from all over and pitched tents until it was a regular tent city. After they took the prisoners out, my job there was to give medicine out to 200 nuns who were living close by. They all had lice. I would say "why can't I see on top of your head.?"

Then Grandpa laughed and said "They wouldn't let me see on top of their head. But they would tell me what they want. …medicine. I would give it to them. What I had to give them was what you would find in a grocery store. I was there with those nuns for 30 days by myself treating them for head lice and anything else they had. I had C rations to eat. It was a little box that had breakfast lunch and dinner. There was a priest there. He would tell me stories. Awful stories. I am not going to tell you about those awful stories, but one thing I want to stress is what this country would have been like if we went through that over here. We could never afford to lose a war over here.

The Japanese took peoples farms, their houses, everything they had. One man was telling me that he had twelve houses and that they paid him for them in Japanese currency. He said he had a whole room full of currency and couldn't buy a loaf of bread. But that is the way they did business. They were cruel."

"I have thought about what would happen if it would have been in this country. I think that many people would have committed suicide. Because they couldn't stand the horror. The people there, they were rough. They live a rough life The little babies, they ate out of a garbage bin. The trucks couldn't dump the garbage for dumping it on those babies. Their stomachs got big and they got worms. Stomach worms. A large white worm the size of a pencil. When they would vomit those worms up it was so sickening. It was awful to think about…that could have happened right here in this country. But I stayed with them, the Army was always giving me the job and leaving me alone with sick people."

"But let me tell you something else. The girls were pretty. The prettiest girls you ever looked at. But if you ever saw them eat it was

Men's Feet Pie

awful. They had old dried fish with flies a blowin. They ate them like a cat. When the whole family would eat, they would have one bowl of rice. The whole family would eat out of that bowl. The would all stick their hands in there and make little wads. And stick it in their jaw. It was quite an experience. I learned a lot of lessons. But I think the main lesson I learned was self-preservation. I had to take care of myself so that I could do for my family, my friends, and my God."

"Then we went on to Santa Rosa. That was 30 miles down past MacArthurs headquarters. We saw him all the time there in the Phillipines. His home was never bothered. In Santa Rosa we had a little hospital there. This is a sad story. I was always up at 5 oclock in the morning. I would get up and go get me some coffee. The guard came in that was in the same tent I was."

"There was an old Filipino lady, she came running in the tent. She says *Japs Japs Japs*. And she pointed to a rice paddy ditch. That crazy guard…I was crazy too, I should never have followed him….he says get your rifle and come on. I didn't know any better. I got my rifle and followed him. He ran up on the bank of that rice paddy ditch and he started shooting at the time that he hit the bank. He says you get down and you stay down and keep my gun loaded. The mound was as hard as a floor. If I could have dug me a hole, I would have but the ground was too hard. I laid there he emptied his gun twice and he took my gun and he emptied it. He killed 5 of em. Five Japanese. They were loaded with dynamite. Can you imagine them coming to that little hospital with a load of dynamite? And they were going to lay in that ditch until it got dark."

"When the shooting was over, I went back to the tent and went to work. There were 7 of them that went into some corn shocks. He shot all seven of them. That was twelve that he shot. It should not have happened that away...they should have been taken prisoners. But the Japs didn't think of taking us prisoners. They were going to kill us. They were loaded with dynamite and they were going to blow up the hospital with all of us in it"

"So we went on back to Manila. This was the time when the war was almost over. They put me in a general hospital with 80 people for me to take care of and give shots and medicine. And we had one guy that pushed the cart. That's all he did. When I came out from work one day, the war was over. I saw a pile of rifles as big as a barn. This was where the Japanese, 45,000 of them come in one day and threw their guns down. I climbed up on that big stack of guns and I saw this one down there and it looked like it was new. I dug down and got it. I took out the firing pin and threw it away. I didn't ever want that gun to be shot."

All of us on the porch thought that the story was over then. The War ended and the guns were thrown down. Grandpa stood up and said "I guess I will be here next Saturday, and I will tell you about when I got to go home."

It happened to be raining that next Saturday, but we all went over to Aunt Darcy's anyway

Men's Feet Pie

because we knew that we would be under her porch. The rain was gentle and it cooled us down from the heat and Grandpa started his going home story.

"I went plumb around the globe. 10,000 miles from San Francisco to New Guinea. Now that was a fair piece. I was 21 years old when I went in and felt like an old man when I got out, but I was glad to be going home alive. We left from Subic Bay. The day I found out it was over, I wasn't excited."

"I thought I should stay to take care of a man. He had a hole in his stomach, and I told the Captain I would stay and take care of him until he got well. The Captain said no, you have been here long enough. I hated to leave him. He was a likeable fellow, but the heat kept him from healing. If we only had ice. We would cover him with a wet sheet and steam would rise off him. I really hated to leave him there like that because I had taken care of him so long. I have wondered many times if he lived long enough to make it home himself.

But, the Captain said no to me staying so I boarded a big ole rusty worn out boat that we took from the depot. They fixed the boat up and it was just fine to carry all the soldiers home. The bunks on the ship were stacked 5 high. 5 guys stacked right on top of each other. When the weather got bad, you got ahold of your bunk and held on. The mess hall would get tore all to pieces. The boat goes through the storms though, even those waves that looked like a green mountain. We kept the hatches closed and no water got in."

"We left about October or November. They

told us that we would all be home for Christmas. I got home on Christmas Eve at 2 in the morning. When I got home, everything was strange to me. I wasn't excited. The Army kept me busy all the time. I wanted to get out, but I wasn't excited about anything."

Willie said "Grandpa, didn't you think about what you were going to do the whole time you were on that ship headed home?"

"Well," said Grandpa, " I did want to be my own boss, then I married your Grandma and I was not ever the boss again."

" I never wanted anyone else telling me what to do….I never thought they were capable. After what I had seen and done, I did not think there was anyone that could be my boss. The guys I was in the Army with, their names come to me instantly. They treated me like I was special. And I still remember each of their names even after all these years and all the things we did to help each other make it out in one piece.

The only reason I am alive today and married your Grandma and had my kids and then my grandchildren is because of those men. So, you all wouldn't even be here if it was not for that one man who kept the Japs from blowing up the hospital I was working in. There was another time that I should have been killed. After treating our own injured, I saw a Jap that we had taken prisoner who had been shot. He was young, no more than a kid, and I felt bad for him. I saw him hurting and I asked the Captain if I could give him some morphine to help him. So, the Captain said yes, I could give him some medicine and when I leaned over to give him a shot, he jumped up and stabbed me. That's how I got this scar on my shoulder. Some of the men I worked with saw it all happen and jumped right in. They took care of me. I was so shocked. I was trying to give him medicine and he stabbed me! The men took care of him and he will never stab anybody again. I owe them my life.

    Bryn asked him if he knew he was going to marry Grandma when he got home.

"I knew your Grandma when I went in. The first 6 months I was in, we never got mail. We were always on the move. Then eventually the letters would catch up. Your Grandma sent me letters and chocolate. The chocolate was always melted in the heat. The letters were censored. They would take a photograph of it and cut it way down, and we got them along time after they were sent. I do wish your Grandma could have sent me some good food. I never understood why the Army did not have more canned food. It was all dehydrated and not very good. We did have beanie weenies, every day three times a day. The food was terrible over there."

"But yes, I knew I would marry your Grandma when I got home if she would have me. I wrote her plenty of letters too. I started every one of the letters I sent to her with "My Dearest Darling." I think she waited on me."

"I came home and bought a car. When I went in, I weighed 116 pounds. I weighed less than that when I came out."

    One day, after I had been home for a couple

of weeks, I was driving down the road to my mom and dad's house and saw a soldier walking. He just got out of the Army. I picked him up and went on driving down the road. I pulled up to the farm and he turned to me and said "are you going here?"

I said "yes".

He stared at me for a minute and said "are you Willie?"

I said "yes."

"Can you believe it. My own brother didn't even know me. I must have sure looked pitiful. I felt pitiful."

"This country can never afford to lose a war. The American people could never go through what those Filipinos went through. Americans are used to such a high standard and I don't think that they could go down to having nothing. No food…no homes. I don't think they could."

Grandpa stood up and stretched his back and looked out towards the garden, The rain had stopped and the story was over. And we would all be eating the good food out of that garden for the rest of the year and I know that we would all remember those stories for the rest of our lives.

That summer of listening to the stories on Aunt Darcy's porch was the best summer. The way Grandpa told his stories made us all feel like we were there with him for just a little bit. I always knew he was strong, even though he was quiet. It makes me wonder if all those times that he was being quiet and not saying anything if he was back in those tents, or thinking about being in a hole while bombs dropped. And the sadness that he had about the war. We never even knew that he had that kind of sadness in him.

Another thing happened because of those stories. By the end of the summer, almost all of the cousins in the family were piled up on Aunt Darcy's porch. That connected us all in a way. Even though we had different parents, we all came from Grandpa and Grandma, and their stories are all part of our stories now.

Whenever I read my books about somebody on an adventure I kind of feel like I am on the adventure with them. Grandpa actually had adventures. A bunch of them. Like with the bears and the mountains and then the jungle, and crossing the ocean on a big ship with a bunch of strangers. He traveled all over the world and saw all those things and did so much. He really didn't seem like the adventuring type, he was so quiet.

I told Grandpa after we heard the last of the stories that he should write a book about it. He just shook his head and said "no, but Sis, maybe you can write up a little something and send it to Readers Digest. Maybe somebody would be interested in it."

Can You Hear the Music

    I don't know how driving can wear you out so much. All you are doing is sitting in the car. But, I had been driving all day and was tense from driving in the snow and being scared of black ice. I had planned on making it to Kansas City, but Topeka was just up the road a way. I saw signs on the interstate for a Motel 6 and decided to go ahead and stop there. This is the first time I had ever checked into a hotel on my own, so I was a little nervous on how it would all work out. It was easy. My dad had already told me on the phone how to do it, and told me to make sure I locked the door as soon as I got in to the room and put a chair in front of the door.

    I got the room key and grabbed my duffle bag and headed in to the hotel. I took a shower and ordered a pizza and pulled out my favorite shirt to sleep in. It was a concert shirt that said AC/DC and was big and comfortable. It was not mine, I never went to that concert, but my best friend Maria had given it to me when I left for college. She was wearing that t-shirt the first day of High School and I loved it. When I looked at myself in that shirt, I started thinking about High School and all of the things that I did during those years.

On the trip from Colorado through Kansas, I had listened to the radio. But for the next part of the trip, I knew that I had to hear my music. I went back out to my car and brought in both of the cases that held all of my cassettes. I plopped down on the bed with my pizza and dumped both of those boxes out to line up the cassettes in the order that I wanted to hear them. That way, when one was finished, I would be able to grab the next one and put it in my tape deck.

Eating my pepperoni pizza while I was looking at my tapes reminded me of the roller rink. That was a food that we always had whenever we went to skate. The music we listened to was Disco. Pure dancing sound and I had a mix tape that Maria and I had made one day.

That was the first tape to go in my box. It had Donna Summer, the BeeGees, Village People and a lot of other good disco sounds. For some reason, Disco always reminded me of Girl Scouts.

I haven't really thought about my Girl Scout days in a long time, which is strange because that was in my life for as long as I can remember. There was a group of about 10 of us that started out as

Brownies, and stayed with it until we were in High School. My mom and another mom were the leaders of the group the whole time. We had a meeting every two weeks and had to wear our uniforms and figure out how to get the badges for our sash. But we did cool things at our meetings. And a lot of them were at the Roller Rink, which was a big deal because we had to drive about 30 miles to get there. All of us would be piled up in the back of the Brown Station Wagon. It was easy to fit 10 brownies in the back of a station wagon, but as we grew and got too big, other moms had to help drive us around.

During this period, our life revolved around the cookie sale and getting to go to Camp Latonka. We never got to go on a big trip when we were brownies, but had to wait until we were *real* Girl Scouts.

But, we got to practice camping in back yards and in make shift tents in the house. We learned to do things like take an empty coffee can and build a fire underneath it. Then you fried a couple of pieces of bacon, just enough to give you good grease and then fry an egg on top. The goal was to fry a perfect egg without breaking the yolk. We did other things to earn badges too, First Aid, Dance, The Arts, and many other things. We did not really know how that we were learning anything, it was all just fun stuff to do.

The best thing about going to the brownie and girl scout meetings was the songs, Of course, we had to learn all of the traditional camp fire songs, or you couldn't get the badge that went on the sash. But we also sang songs that were on the radio at the time. And the radio was full of disco .

There was one time that we had a real adventure and had to actually use the stuff we learned. We were newly graduated from Brownie to Girl Scout when mom and the other leader decided to take us on a nature hike so that we could collect items for our nature badge.

We went up the levee by the River and took a long road back on the river bottoms. We all had assembled little back packs with lunch and first aid items, ropes, and bug spray. We had little pads and pencils and were supposed to draw and document any animal we saw and take notes about the trees and other plants we saw while we watched out for poison ivy.

We had a blast. It is amazing when you walk in the bottoms, because there is another world that you don't know exists. All of us had ridden along that Levee our whole lives and whenever you looked, you just saw trees, and an occasional deer.

But when you are actually *In the Trees* and walking through them, you see a whole different world. We came upon a big black snake that was in the middle of eating a frog. It's mouth was full so we knew that it couldn't eat us, but we did not stay long to look at it. We kept walking further and further in and stopped occasionally to put on some bug spray and sketch a few trees. We all felt like grand adventurers. At one point, the trees kind of opened up and there was a big area that was full of ferns and a bunch of plants but the ground was getting soggy.

As we walked, the ground got softer and softer and then started sticking to our shoes. My Mom was walking in front of us all and moving the plants with her stick to make sure there weren't any poisonous snakes and all of a sudden she yelled for us to stop.

We stopped, and right in front of my eyes, my mom started to get smaller. She had stepped into a patch of gumbo or something and was sinking. She tried to get unstuck and the more she tried to get out, the deeper she went. The other leader was at the back of our group and came running up to see what was going on. Then she started to sink too, but she wised up quick and got out of it. By this time, the girls knew that there was real trouble, because my Mom was yelling "Oh Shit! It's going to take a crane to get me out of here!"

I kind of froze and did not know what to do as I watched my Mom struggle, then one of the other girls threw out a rope to my mom, but it didn't reach. So, all of us got out our ropes and tied them together and threw it to my mom and we somehow managed to drag her out of that gumbo. W could never have gotten her out if it had not been for one of the girls who crawled on her belly and used her hands to scoop mud out from around my mom's legs.

We tugged her in like she was a fish on the end of a line and when she could finally stand up, she was so covered in gumbo and mud and plants on the bottom half of her body that she couldn't walk. We were all covered up in that mud by the time we got her pulled in and had some scrapes of our own. We tried wiping it off of her, but that was not working, so my Mom stripped her clothes off right there in the bottoms and we all walked back to the station wagon covered in that stinking mud.

When we finally made it back to the road, we tried washing off with the canteens of water, which did no good at all. It just kind of mixed in with the mud. Finally, the other leader said lets all just go to the car wash because we can't take these kids back to their houses like this. So, all of us newly graduated from Brownie to Girl Scouts went to the car wash and took turns hosing each other off and when that was done, we took turns putting on bandaids and calamine lotion and bandaging each other up. Of course, most of the injuries didn't require ace bandages, but if there was even a little mark on someone they got wrapped up. When it was all over, we got back into the station wagon and mom turned up the radio and we all belted out Gloria Gaynor singing "I will Survive." That kind of became our song after that day.

Missouri

    I woke up in the hotel the next morning, with my tapes lined up and got the car packed up and ready to go. Made a collect call home to my dad to let him know I was leaving and I was on the way.

    I had my tape already in and playing as I pulled out on to the highway and jammed with the BeeGees until I hit Kansas City then switched over to Journey.

    When I put that tape in, my mind went right back to High School. The first day of school started and I was terrified. My whole life, I had gone to school with the same kids every year and there were only 12 of us in my graduating class at Immaculate Conception. We always stayed in one room with

Men's Feet Pie

the same teacher for all of the subjects. All of our books were kept in our own desk, and you always knew what to expect with the routines of the day. Plus, you always wore a uniform and everybody looked the same.

Life was different in High School. There were 300 kids in my grade. And I didn't know any of them. My friends that I had were all in different classes than me and we occasionally saw each other walking down the hallway. Most of the students were bussed in from other towns where they had all gone to small schools. It did not occur to me that everyone must have felt the same way. You would think that with all of those kids, you would never feel lonely. But I did.

Eventually that changed, as we got to know each other and found out that we were really all just small town kids that got thrown together. There were certain groups and you knew who was who by what music they listened to and you knew that by what bands were on their t shirts. I still liked to read in High School, but that got taken over by music.

For one thing, I got a sound system for my birthday. It had a tape deck, a record player, and two speakers that were each about three feet tall. We kept it in the living room next to my dad's aquarium. There was even a spot inside the cabinet to keep all of the cassette tapes in. So, instead of saving up money for books, I started saving up for my favorite cassette tapes. Records and 8 tracks were a thing of the past. The first tape I bought on my own was Journey and my favorite song on that tape was "Wheel in the Sky." I must have rewound that tape a hundred times to listen to that song over and over again.

So, as I crossed the state line from Kansas to Missouri, I was singing at the top of my lungs right along with Steve Perry and the rest of the band and thankful to finally be back in my own state. I listened to the songs I wanted on that tape then pulled out the next one. The band was Kansas and I probably should have listened to it first since I just came from Kansas, but Journey will always be my first pick of the music from high school days.

Singing about Wayward Sons and cruising down that highway that led me home, I saw the billboards that said "Welcome to Missouri, and the Show-Me State. They showed the state symbol and flag. I wish that Missouri had a state smell. If it did, it would have to be honeysuckle because that smell is home to me.

Anyway, I jammed to Kansas and watched my speed and got lost in thinking about high school. It did not take long for me to make new friends. I got involved in sports and quiz bowl and played the clarinet in the marching band. Our band was the best one in the state. There were about 200 kids in the band and when the drum line started playing, I would feel so full of pride that it felt like my heart was going to jump right out of my chest.

The days of wearing a uniform to school were forgotten and I stressed out every day on what to wear. Maria and I went to the drug store and got set up with our supplies. My hair was so big. And it all started with *Gee, Your Hair Smells Terrific*. I had a great perm and so did all of my friends and Aqua Net Hairspray became my best friend in the morning. Then, before I could leave the house, a good spritz with Loves Baby Soft Mist and I was ready to take on the world.

The everyday part of school days are still kind of a blur, but some things I remember just like they were yesterday. The best part of being in high school was the weekends. When I was 15, my dad finally let me go and circle town with my friends. Of course, Maria and I were inseparable still and we had our group that we hung out with. But the weekends were full with riding around on Friday and Saturday night, and we all thought we were so cool.

Sunday at Grandma's for dinner never changed. I didn't have to pretend to be cool there. We still read our books after dinner.

I had a secret kind of music that I liked and didn't tell anyone but Maria about it. When I told her, she said she liked it too, but never told anyone. It was the Carpenters and they just did not fit in with Def Leppard and Boston, so we hid that tape in my glove box and only pulled it out when were riding around by ourselves. So, we would ride around and sing to the top of our lungs about being on the Top of the World and Lookin Down on Creation but as soon as we pulled up to the Chat N Chew where our friends were parked, , we would snatch the cassette tape out of the player and put in a different tape. Maria was like that, she was popular, and one of the cool ones, but she did uncool things with me. I loved her for that. I don't really think she liked the Carpenters all that much but she still sang it with me.

My family at home was pretty much the same. Willie was still quoting commercials though and drove us all nuts whenever we tried to watch a show. But, we were used to it so it was not really that big of a deal.

I was a Junior when my sister Bobbie Sue went to high School and things really got exciting at home. She was always in a mood of some sorts. And everything Mom and Dad did embarrassed her. For one thing, my parents went through this phase of having to wear matching clothes. Mom ordered them from Sears or Montgomery Ward and they had about 4 sets of matching outfits. Whenever we had a ball game or something, they would always dress alike and Bobbie Sue would go to pieces and act like they weren't there.

I don't think that I have mentioned that my family on my dad's side was Polish. His mom was actually born in Poland. I think that is kind of cool. My dad did something that my sister always hated. He would call her by a Polish name when she was younger. Bobatchka. At least I think it was Polish for Bobbie Sue. She hated it, and always said not to call her that.

It really didn't turn in to a problem until she got in high School. And the madder she got whenever he called her that only made him do it more. Especially in front of her friends. She would come rolling into the house with her friends and dad would say Bobatchka, have you got your room cleaned up? He did not really care about her room, but he loved to call her that because it made her so mad.

As bad as she hated it when Mom and Dad wore matching outfits, she hated it even more whenever my dad wore his one-piece polyester jump suit. He had two of them. One was bright yellow and the other one was sky blue.

Other parents wore matching outfits a lot, so it was kind of common, but nobody wore a jump suit like my dad. They had one zipper in the front from the bottom up to the top and always stopped just about half way up his chest, so his hairy chest was showing.

She would roll her eyes whenever he would put one of those on and he would say "Bobatchka, you got something to say to me?" Then she would walk off in a huff. Dad would just laugh and flex his muscles and tell her he would give her a knuckle sammich if she kept it up.

My sister and I got along pretty well while we were both in high school. Of course, she was younger so we did not see each other much. I was in the band and she was a cheerleader. We shared our magazines, Teen Beat and Tiger Beat. We both pulled out our favorite posters to hang on the wall in the bedroom we still shared. I had Scott Baio to look at and she had Shaun Cassidy. We never shared our clothes when she got in high school.

I was kind of plain when it came to clothes and usually just wore jeans and a t shirt, but she dressed fancy. My dad always said that he could not believe that his daughters were so different. One like to eat fancy food and the other liked to wear fancy clothes. There was one time that I did borrow her shoes to go out in. I had to practically beg to borrow those penny loafers but I was going to be circling town with my friends for my 16th birthday and for some reason I wanted to wear them. She finally said yes, and I got all fixed up and went out. It was going to be a great night. I got some cassettes for my birthday and a new case to put them all in. Reo Speedwagon, Boston, Styx, and John Cougar.

Maria, Leslie, and a bunch of other friends picked me up and out came the tapes and our Saturday night got started. They said that they had some surprises for me.

I think that the devil must have made Sloe Gin. I only say that because when I took my first drink, it tasted really good mixed in with the 7-UP I just got at the Chat N Chew. I can't believe how easy it is to get drunk, but when something tastes that good you don't even think about it.

Of course, I had only tasted beer before and that was just a little sip and I hated the way it tasted. We were circling town in Leslie's mustang. John Cougar was blaring and we were singing "Hurt So Good" and the next thing I knew, I got dizzy. I told Leslie to pull over to the side of the levee so I could pee and the next thing I knew I couldn't walk. They took me home and dropped me off on the front steps and then my Dad opened the door.

He looked at me and started hollering for mom who came out of the kitchen to find me leaning on the door. The next thing I know I was puking all over my sisters shoes that she let me wear. I don't really remember that night, but the next morning when I got up, my mom was standing over my bed and told me to get a shower because Grandma wanted to see me.

My head....oh did my head hurt. But as bad as I felt, when I knew that I was going to have to face my Grandma, I hurt even worse. I wish that we could have kept just this one little thing from her, but in our family it was impossible. Grandma knew everything when it happened. And if she did not know, as soon as you saw her, you felt like you had to tell her about it. It was like she could read your mind so you just might as well go on and tell her about it.

So, I got cleaned up and my mom took me over to Grandma's house and dropped me off. She did not say one word to me on the way, but as soon as we pulled up to the house, she started yelling that they thought that they were going to have to take me to the hospital to get my stomach pumped because they thought I had taken some drugs.

"And, we want to know who bought you the booze because your dad is going to kick somebody's ass today." I did not tell where we got it from. I wanted to tell the truth, but I did not want my dad to kill anybody that day so I just said "I don't know." Mom yelled a little more about me "being the example and both my sister and little brother saw me drunk and stumbling around and puking everywhere and that was going to be my punishment....knowing that they saw me like that. I already felt bad enough and then that guilt got added on and I just did not know how I was going to face Grandma.

But, I went in and Grandpa was sitting in his chair chewing on a cigar and watching tv. I could tell he did not know anything about it. So I walked back in to the kitchen because I could smell food cooking. Grandma was standing at her counter making chicken and dumplins. She looked up and smiled and just shook her head. Then she rummaged around in her cabinet and brought out some alka seltzer and made me a glass.

She watched me drink it down and then told me to get the eggs out of the fridge. It was time to make the dough. I brought the eggs over and sat at the counter so I could watch her work the dough. It was like watching magic happen. Sometimes I wondered how a sack full of raw stuff could turn into something that filled the house with a good smell and could make everybody so happy. She always boiled the hens for a couple of hours until the meat would fall off of the bones. Then she would take out a couple of glasses full of the broth and set it aside to cool.

She had already cooled down the broth, so she got out a sack of flour and dumped it right on the counter. While she was sprinkling salt and pepper on it she asked me how my birthday party went with my friends. I told her "it went just fine until I started drinking Sloe Gin. I didn't know it would taste so good and get you drunk."

She fluffed all the flour up until it made a white powdery mountain. Then she put a hole in the top of the powder. She said "Well, I guess you learned that lesson the hard way. Sometimes that is the only way it really sinks in. But you were lucky your friends took you home instead of some boy that would take advantage of you." I just nodded.

She got out two bowls and started cracking open the eggs. She separated the yolks in to one bowl and the whites in to another. Then, she set aside the whites because she will use that for the meringue on the lemon and chocolate pies later.

The broth has cooled down by this time so she whipped the eggs in with the broth and then slowly poured a little in to the hole in the flour. She pushed the flour over in to the liquid and starts pressing it down, push in more flour and then add more liquid. She has done this so many times that she doesn't even have to think about it. As she was mixing things up she talked to me. I watched her hands while she worked. Her hands had freckles and scars and short fingernails. They pushed and pulled and before too long, the white powder had mixed perfectly with the liquid and what was before us was a golden lump of dough that was going to become chicken and dumplins.

She got out her marble rolling pin from the big crock on the edge of the counter. She scraped the counter top smooth with a silver spatula and then threw down a fine layer of flour and started to roll out the dough. She rolled and then flipped it over, added a little more flour and kept on rolling until it was just right.

While all this was going on, she was telling me about the book she was reading and what Aunt Darcy had been up to that week. I was waiting for her to get me. Yell or something. Her being this nice to me was only making things worse. It reminded me of when we were little kids and did something wrong and she would tell us to go out to the yard and get a switch because we were going to get a whipping.

We would pick our switches and be in tears the whole time we were looking for one. In the door we would go and hand her our switch and she would just look at it and tell us it was not good enough to give anyone a proper whipping. So, "take it back outside and come back to get something to eat and just remember next time to get a good switch" because she "would not waste her time whipping us with a switch that wasn't going to work."

Me and my sister and brother and cousins must have picked up hundreds of switches over the years to take in to Grandma and I don't remember her ever whipping any of us. It was always punishment enough that she even told us to go get one.

So, I was waiting for it then she said, "I imagine that your mom and dad are going to punish you pretty bad for this. So, I am not going to make you go get a switch." When she said that, I started crying and laughing at the same time. How does she do that? Always know what is going through your mind. I told her that mom said that I was not going to get to drive for the first whole month of my 16 birthday, even though I had just got my driver's license.

She just nodded and then pulled out the paring knife and cut long strips in the dough and then diagonals the other way and what was left looked like a quilt on the counter. She sprinkled flour over the top of the whole thing and she fluffed it up to let it dry for an hour or so.

    Then she made some space on the counter and said that it was time for me to learn how to make meringue for the pies. So, Grandma made me another alka seltzer and taught me how to make meringue all afternoon.

I am so glad to be back in Missouri. The drive so far seems to have taken forever. But now, the miles are going so fast and I know that I will be home in a couple of hours. This whole drive I have been thinking about my family and what life was life when I was little. Now that I am 18 years old and a grown up, I see things a little differently. After I got off being punished for getting drunk, I started driving everywhere. And that is when I really started learning to be an adult.

I took the kids places and got to go to the store and run errands for my mom. I used to sound just like my mom when I was yelling for the kids to get their heads back in the windows and stop spilling sodas in my car. My dad liked for me to drive the kids around because then he did not have to. He did set down some rules though. One of those rules came about from me driving the kids to the IGA to pick up bread and milk.

It was during the summer after I turned 16. We all went barefooted most of the time in the house, and it was almost impossible to get the little kids to put on shoes whenever we went somewhere. So, I told Willie, Bryn, and Zack to get in the car and did not bother with fighting to get shoes on. We were only going to be in the store for a few

Men's Feet Pie

minutes and kids went in there barefoot all the time anyway, and so did a lot of adults. I pulled up to the IGA and everybody tumbled out and in we went.

We saw Irene that day. She pretended not to see us. She still looked the same with her drawn on eyebrows and big juicy lips. Her hair was a different color but that was about the only difference. She saw us coming while she was getting a grocery cart and fumbled around in her purse for a minute and got out her cigarettes and lit one up before she started shopping. Off she went, flicking ashes all over the place. We didn't get a cart, but as we walked down the aisles, I just filled up the kids hands with the stuff we needed. Of course, everybody we saw in the store that day knew us and we had to stop and talk. It was only polite. We got our food and left to go home and the kids all walked in to the house with the stuff. Dad was there messing around with his aquariums and we went to turn on the tv and plop down on the couch when my dad looked up. The boys had taken up spots on the floor in front of the TV and were just laying there. I saw my dad staring at their feet and he said "What is all over your feet?

We did not know what he was talking about.

Then he shook his head in disgust. "Grocery store feet!"

"I did not raise my kids to run around all over town with filth caked on the bottom of their feet." "Sis, you are the oldest and know better than to take the kids into the store without shoes on!"

I still did not know what he was talking about. I told him that. Then he threw a real fit. I didn't really know what the big deal was because everybody ran around barefoot in the summer. I found out that the grocery store left its own kind of dirt when I took the kids to the bathroom to wash their feet. I could not even scrape that grime off.

I don't really know what that dirt was made of. The smooth floors looked clean, but they weren't. I guess when we walked all over the store, the dirt made some sort of plastic because it was stuck to the bottom of their feet and I figured that it was there to stay. When I thought about it, I guessed it was because of all the ashes people flicked off their cigarettes while they shopped. You would think that the grocery store would have some ash trays up and down the aisles, but they didn't. Anyway, the important thing is that I learned about grocery store feet and that I was to never ever let the kids run around barefoot in the IGA again.

Another thing that happened when I got to drive was that I got to go look at the River anytime I felt like it. My sister was always bugging me to take her and her friends to circle town just like the older kids did. So, I took them.

Most of the time, Maria was with me and Bobbie Sue and her friends would be in the back seat. Those girls were a couple of years younger than us and always wanted to circle town the same way. First stop was at the Chat N Chew to get a drink and after that was taken care of, we would make two circles in town and then up to the Levee. We had to ride that Levee looking at the River while they listened to their favorite song. They had this routine all worked out. Maria knew and had the cassette ready to turn up the Doobie Brothers singing Old Black Water. Each girl had their part that they sang and then all together they would sing about old black water …keep on rolling….Mississippi moon keep on shining….Then, at the end of the song the car practically shook with them all singing about funky Dixie land pretty momma come and take me by the hand.

So, whenever I hear the Doobie Brothers, I think about riding that Levee with them all singing.

My sister and my mom had a lot of arguments whenever Bobbie Sue went to High School. They would argue over anything, and it was usually my sister picking the fight. Mostly it was a lot of slammed doors and eye rolling, but there was one time that Bobbie Sue took it too far.

My Mom always crossed her legs together and did a little curtsy every time she sneezed. A curtsy just like you would give to the Queen, if we had a queen. In the family it was called the death of a thousand curtsies because it never happened in one sneeze. Once she got started, it seemed to go on forever. The fit usually started with her twitching her nose, trying to fight the inevitable.

Then it would start. First sneeze…..the legs would clamp together like a giant vise clamp. Then her back would arch and she would throw her head back so far it seemed like her head would spontaneously detach from the rest of her body. Then her head would snap forward and the spasms would start. They were accompanied by sound, of course, but a sound that is not found anywhere else in nature. It would start something like this uh uh uh Uh UH UUH UUHH tu. The tu part of that in the beginning was somewhere in the medium to high range on the voice scale , then it would start coming faster and faster, each time the sounds would crescendo and the timing would become shorter and shorter until it came out as *etu,* the sound I would expect a French poodle to make if it spoke.

By the time she got to the fourth or fifth sneeze the pitch would be so high that it would shatter glass. When it started, it was hard to look away,. Kind of like watching a train wreck. It was horrible, because her face would get redder and redder until it finally turned a deep shade of purple. The throwing back and forward of her head was an expansive motion in the beginning, but as the sneezes came faster and faster and the sounds would become shorter and shorter until she was a mass of vise gripped legs holding up a quivering torso and a purple head.

Finally, when the sneezes were all played out, or her poor quivering body could take no more, they would end. She would slowly uncross her legs and stretch her neck. Everybody who witnessed it would look away, not wanting her to know that they had just seen one of the most horrific sights in their life. Then everybody would pretend it didn't happen.

There was a certain perfume that would always set it off. My sister came home wearing that perfume one day and it sent Mom into a frenzy of curtsy sneezing fits. From that day forward she was not allowed to wear that perfume. This perfume just so happened to be my sisters favorite and she couldn't bear to throw it away because it was expensive and she liked to smell expensive. She also liked to look expensive and she even tried to talk expensive. I was surprised that she even agreed to put it up but as much as she liked to smell expensive, she was mortified every time the curtsies happened.

So, she hid the perfume and swore that the day she moved out she was going to use it as air freshener in her very own apartment. That's another thing about her, she always wanted to live in an apartment,.....like it was so rich to have an apartment.

Once, mom was up for this award and it was in the newspaper and everything. There was going to be a big deal happening at the Jaycee Hall and everybody in town was going to be there. Well, Bobbie Sue and mom got into this really vicious fight because my sister wanted to date one of the Cloony brothers. Everybody in town knew that no good ever came from dating a Cloony.

The boys in that family always got girls pregnant and the Cloony sisters always got into fights. Well, after this argument with mom, Bobbie Sue stalked out of the house and said that she wasn't going to the awards banquet and with a bunch of dumb hicks. Dad walked in and told her to get her ass back in the house or she wouldn't have an ass left.

Mom was late for the banquet, but then, she was late for everything anyway so no one was really surprised. Mom and dad took off so that she could be there in time for her award and I was supposed to bring Bobbie Sue as soon as she got ready.

Well, after mom and dad left to go to the banquet, she dug out her bottle of perfume. She knew that mom had to give a speech when she got her award. So she sprayed this perfume all over herself and had a wicked smile on her face when she left. I knew that this would be trouble but Bobbie Sue refused to wash it off.

When she got to the banquet she waited to talk to mom until just before the names were called to go to the podium. She then walked up to mom and told mom how sorry she was about the fight. Well, mom started smiling and reached out to give her a big hug. She was smiling and then she got this kind of sick look on her face. At that moment the announcer called mom's name to come up and get her award. That is when the curtsies started.

Now, some of the women in the audience had witnessed this before at the Beauty Shop, but most were new to this sort of thing.

Mom's legs clamped together. The announcer started saying things about the family...then her head flew back and the curtsy started full force. It got really quiet in the Jaycee Hall until mom was all finished. It seemed to last forever. Her hair, which she prided herself on, was sticking up all over the place and her face was red and the new mascara she bought just for this event was not waterproof so it was running down her face in black streams. But, she was classy. She walked right up to the mike and gave her speech just as if nothing was wrong and she didn't look like she just came in from a tornado.

When dad found out what happened he came roaring in to the house and was screaming for Bobbie Sue. He grabbed a hold of her and shook her and told her he was gonna bust that bottle of perfume over her head if she ever pulled another stunt like that again. Mom didn't talk to her for two weeks.

They were always having trouble like that. It seemed like the nicer mom was to my sister, the meaner she was to mom. Mom would usually let her get away with it, but Dad never would.

My sister and I really did not start getting along until I was getting ready to leave for college. After I graduated from High School, I had the whole summer to run around with my friends and by this time Bobbie Sue had calmed down a little bit. That summer was so exciting. I got a scholarship to go to college in Colorado and could not wait to get out of the little town I grew up in. In fact, I figured that once I left, I would only come back for holidays. I was ready to go out and have my own adventures and SEE THE WORLD, just like Grandma wanted me to. There was only one thing that happened that made me think that I should not move so far away.

It was the end of the summer before I was supposed to leave for college when Grandma had to go to the hospital. We were all worried because we never thought that she would have to go to the hospital for anything. She was in there for a couple of days because she had a mild heart attack. Me and Bobbie Sue drove up to see her and walked in to her room just in time to see the nurses changing out her catheter bag. Grandma looked at the nurse and said "is that what you make the coffee with because it tastes like piss?"

Then she looked over and saw me and Bobbie Sue and said, "get my pocketbook will you, I need you to go to somewhere and get me a real cup of coffee."

We felt a little sorry for the nurse, because Grandma was cranky but we couldn't help but laugh. She wanted some real coffee, so we went to get her some. When we got back to the room, Aunt Darcy was there. Grandma was sleeping. So, I whispered to Aunt Darcy and said that we brought her real coffee but that we weren't going to wake her up. That is when Grandma opened her eyes and said, "don't worry girls. I am not ready to leave you the family heirlooms just yet."

Bobbie Sue said "what do you mean, heirlooms? Like the kind of things that are passed down from generation to generation?"

Grandma said "Yes. Those things." Then Grandma snorted and said "every woman in our family gets the same thing when they turn about 40 years old. So you know that you have something to look forward to."

Bobbie Sue walked closer to Grandma and asked "can you tell us what it is right now so we know?"

Grandma looked at us both real serious and then looked at Aunt Darcy and said "do you want to tell them or should I?"

Aunt Darcy said "I will let you tell them. " So, with Grandma laying in that hospital bed and Aunt Darcy sitting right beside her they both got really quiet and Grandma said "when you both turn 40 you will get something that has been passed down for every single generation to all the women in the family. It is a big butt, big boobs, and a bad temper!" Then they both started laughing and that is when we knew that Grandma was going to be ok.

Almost There

    I was driving through St. Louis when I pulled out the only cassette tape I had of Elvis Presley. I had to listen to this music because it is my Grandma's favorite. She had a special connection to Elvis because she used to work at RCA Victor in the 1950s and pressed his records. That was way before cassette tapes came out. It was before he really became famous so she felt like she was part of him making it big. She even had a bunch of those old records at her house.

    My favorite song was Suspicious Minds, but I have heard all of his songs at one time or another at Grandma's. She loved Hound Dog and Jailhouse Rock and we would have that music on all the time while we were cooking. Another one I liked was In the Ghetto, even though it was a sad song.

Men's Feet Pie

One day that I will always remember was the day of sadness in town. It was August 16, 1977. Elvis Presley died that day.

Everybody in town was in shock. It was all anybody talked about, and his music was playing on all the radios. It hit my Grandma really hard. It was like the world stopped for a minute. Nobody could believe it and when I saw Grandma that day, she told me the story of her making those records. She acted like he was a member of our family. The way she talked about him and his movies and how important he was to the world made me wish that I had met him, just once. While she was telling me about him and his story of finding love with Priscilla, she just shook her head and said "I think we all died a little today. There will never be anybody like him again. His music changed the world. "

So, for two hours, I listened to Elvis and rewound the tape over and over again until I got closer to home.

.

Home

Even though I have been driving for days, when I pulled in to town, I automatically started driving the circle. And then straight to the River. I drove down Main Street and up and over the levee and down to my sacred spot. And then I couldn't control it anymore. I saw that water and my Grotto and lost it. The tears started coming and wouldn't stop. I finally pulled over to the side and walked down the side of the levee to the Grotto.

Ducking in under the doorway, I took big gulps of that muddy water smell. I looked out over that big water and thanked God that I was finally home. Now, I'm here, I'm home. But I have to get to Grandma's house. Everyone will be there. I don't want to walk through that door but I have to go. I'm surely out of tears by now, especially after the falling apart I just did. But, I don't have another choice. I walked back up the levee, gave the River another look and got in my car.

Grandma's house was only about 2 blocks away, and I could see that cars lined the street on both sides. Some people were leaving and others were coming in and carrying in dishes of food. It seems odd to think of food in Grandma's house and she has not cooked any of it. It seems so wrong somehow.

I want to throw all of that food into the yard and kick everyone out. All I really want right now is a big pot of her chicken and dumplins and for her to be standing at the stove whipping mashed potatoes.

I feel kind of numb. Like this day isn't real. But I know it is when my dad comes outside to meet me. He says "did you have any trouble on the road?", then without waiting for my answer, he says "your momma is having a real bad time right now."

Then some woman I don't even know says "honey, I am so sorry for your loss" and I lose it right there in the yard in front of everybody. I walked in and it hit me when she did not come to the door. She's gone.

What are we going to do without her? And how are we possibly going to make it through Christmas this year, which is only three weeks away. She left us right before her holiday. I can't even bring myself to say the word "died."

I am having all of these thoughts and remembering when she called me a woman, and remembering helping her make peach fried pies and us reading Harlequin Romance novels and thinking all these thoughts about me and Grandma, then I see Grandpa sitting in the chair. He has a towel around his neck, and every so often, he pulls it right over his head and won't talk to anyone.

He heard my voice, and pulled it off long enough to tell me what I already knew. She is gone and we are never going to be the same.

I don't know how we made it through that day, the day of visitation when everyone in town came over to their house. I was not surprised at the number of people, but I was surprised at some of the ones who did show up, because they had a bad name in town.

I overheard my dad thanking this one man for coming, and he said that when he got out of prison, he did not have any food in his house and was probably going to end up going back in for shoplifting food. He was standing in the grocery aisle, wondering how he could get out with a loaf of bread and some peanut butter when Grandma saw him. She must have known what he was about to do and she made him get a shopping cart and she bought him a whole cart full of groceries and then told him where he could get a job for good cash money working for a farmer she knew. It was one of her brothers.

He said that he would never forget that woman and that she probably saved him from going back to a life of crime. He never did really thank her, but he had to come and show his respects.

I think that we should cancel Christmas this year. It came a lot faster than it usually did. The days kind of ran in to each other and Christmas got closer and closer. Dad tried to make everything normal, because mom was not in any shape to do it.

And Grandpa was just lost. But he said that Grandma would have wanted everybody to have Christmas and that she was smiling down on us from Heaven.

Grandma was the leader of our family. And without her, nobody really knew how to act. I have heard people talk about how the men are the head of the household, but in our family, Grandma was the head of all the households in some way. I saw my mom go to the phone one day to call Grandma about something and while she was dialing the numbers she just lost it and started crying right there in the kitchen. She forgot that she was gone.

Christmas morning rolled around, and we tried to make everything normal. Mom got up early to watch everybody go to their piles of gifts left by Santa. She smiled, but every so often a tear would slide down her face and she would wipe it away real fast. I think she was glad when opening presents time was over because we had to go to the kitchen to start getting the meal together because everybody in the family was coming over at noon. Of course, the aunts all brought a dish but nobody even attempted to make chicken and dumplins. We would do without those for the first time ever. I think the thought of eating dumplins made by someone other than Grandma was just too much to bear. So we did without. But we had plenty of other food.

When dessert time came around, right there on the big table we always kept dessert on were two big Mince Meat Pies, all covered with whipped topping. When mom saw those she looked quickly at Aunt Darcy, who was shocked too. Mom said "Darcy did you make those?" Aunt Darcy said "no, I did not!"

So mom and Aunt Darcy asked around to all of the aunts to see who brought those pies. Nobody knew and they don't remember seeing them when they were putting their desserts on the table. It was a mystery to everyone in the family of how those pies got on the table, or even in the house for that matter.

Mom finally decided that it didn't matter how they got there and I watched her face as she cut out the first slice out. She started laughing when a plastic foot came out of the edge of the piece. It was the first time she had laughed since the day we lost Grandma. She cut more pieces and plated them up while we all watched. While she was slicing, she started talking about that mess and Willie and the first year the Men's Feet Pie came about and how Grandma used to laugh about that day whenever she told one of her friends about it.

Then Aunt Darcy laughed and told about the time with the Goat Cheese and wondered how, still to this day, Grandma managed to swallow that cheese to keep from offending her. Pretty soon, everybody was telling a Grandma story while they ate that pie. Every so often, someone would yell "I got one!" whenever they found a plastic body part.

While all of this was going on, I snuck a look over at Bryn. She was trying so hard not to smile, and she finally looked over at me. She just gave me a little nod and we both knew that from now on, we were the ones that were going to keep

Men's Feet Pie

that tradition in the family going on. The day before Christmas Eve, we both took some of our Christmas money and went to the drug store and bought up all the plastic toys that had feet one them. I'm sure the clerk thought we were nuts when we said "nope, that one is connected" or this one's feet are too big to fit in the pie.

While everyone was out shopping and at work, we got into that kitchen and made those pies, and then hid them up in the closet right next to my Little House Books, which were still stored there. Some things, even if they don't make any sense to others need to be kept going in a family if it keeps a memory alive. Baking those pies in the kitchen was hard in the beginning, but I imagined Grandma there telling us how to do it. And so I told Bryn the steps just like Grandma was whispering it in my ear, reminding me of all the times I had helped her make them before.

While we were rolling out the crust, Bryn told me how sorry she was for ruining my book that day. I had forgiven her years ago and told her that. She said that she always felt bad whenever she thought about it. I guess you never know what is on a person's mind until they tell you. Anyway, that was an important day, because I really felt like I was doing something important….you know….keeping Grandma alive with us on Christmas by making her favorite pie. And teaching Bryn.

Bryn never cared much about cooking but I think that day in the kitchen making those pies changed her somehow. I never really thought about it, but it was not that I liked cooking so much as I liked to be in the kitchen with other people, and all of us cooking together.

Like Mom and Aunt Darcy, and especially Grandma. Maybe I'm crazy, but I think that the food you make hears you laughing and talking while you make it and that is what makes it taste so good. Maybe that was Grandma's secret ingredient all those years.

After the Christmas dinner was cleaned up, my Mom and I sat in the kitchen while we shared the last piece of the Men's Feet Pie. It seemed like something had released all the sadness that we had in us since the day of Grandma's funeral. For three weeks, we had all waited for that first Christmas without her to come and go and now it was time for us to get on with our lives. Even though we didn't quite know how to do that.

Mom asked me if I wanted to stay home and get a job or if I planned on going back to Colorado. I took the last bite of pie and asked her what she thought I should do.

Earlier that morning, I had no plans to ever leave my family again. But with the letting go of the sadness something had changed. My mom told me that I was the only one who could make that decision, but if Grandma was sitting at the table with us she would tell me to go SEE THE WORLD. So that is what I did.

Men's Feet Pie

CPSIA information can be obtained
at www.ICGtesting.com
Printed in the USA
LVHW082146070322
712875LV00027B/668